# Midnight
# Meanders

# Midnight Meanders

Annika Sheinbach Jensen

**LODESTONE BOOKS**

Winchester, UK
Washington, USA

First published by Lodestone Books, 2014
Lodestone Books is an imprint of John Hunt Publishing Ltd., Laurel House, Station Approach,
Alresford, Hants, SO24 9JH, UK
office1@jhpbooks.net
www.johnhuntpublishing.com

For distributor details and how to order please visit the 'Ordering' section on our website.

Text copyright: Annika Sheinbach Jensen 2013

ISBN: 978 1 78279 412 7

A CIP catalogue record for this book is available from the British Library.

Design: Stuart Davies
www.stuartdaviesart.com

Printed in the USA by Edwards Brothers Malloy

We operate a distinctive and ethical publishing philosophy in all
areas of our business, from our global network of authors to
production and worldwide distribution.

To Reid, for seeing me through this,
To John, for opening my eyes,
And to William, for giving me a name.

# PREFACE

This is a book. It is a book written by a hopeful part-time author and full-time high school student; it is a book that you might relate to, or one that you might just enjoy having around. It is one that has accompanied long nights of insomnia and seen me from all angles, one filled with the remnants of my best days and my worst. It is a first-hand observation of ordinary adolescence and extraordinary people, and it is a reminder that not everything is grim. This is a book for those who need a companion in lonely times, those who have found happiness, those who are wandering and those who just really like books. This book is one that would not have seen its conclusion without the support of a crazy family, a few quirky teachers, some goofy horses, a cool dude from Texas, a future secret agent who loves literature just as much as I do, and the beautiful members of B'raisheet BBG; it is the result of seventeen years of eclectic inspiration and it will hopefully serve a similar purpose to whoever is kind enough to read it. This is a book, and I am truly thankful that you decided to open it.

Annika

# ONE

The fluorescent shine from the overhead street light danced on the curb of the road, skidding off the gathered rainwater and bouncing back up to the dark velvet sky. It was around forty-five degrees and misting, weather that William seemed to thrive in, and he felt himself smiling as he turned a corner and walked down another sleeping street, grey hood pulled up over his head.

Springtime in Maryland was spectacular. Those who cared enough to plant cherry blossom trees would boast about how lovely their yards looked when the satin pink and white petals bloomed. The grass turned its preferred shade of green. It rained. The weather evened out and settled into its perfect glory, a snug fit of just between forty and sixty degrees daily. There were good feelings, fruit, the Stanley Cup Playoffs, and in general it felt like a big gust of pleasantness had just blown in from the south. This night was particularly good.

William padded lightly down the sidewalk, parallel to the deserted street lined with a protective buffer of trees that always stood on guard to keep the sleepy suburban neighborhood safe, their branches stretched out like spears, ready to fight. William slipped his hands into his pockets. He looked ragged in his old grey hoodie and sweatpants, big headphones taped up at the sides from overuse and excess of love. His music was playing softly, barely noticeable; just a background tune that you might hear in movies as a young, naïve teenager was casually walking down the street. However, most young, naïve teenagers did not casually walk down the street at one o'clock in the morning.

It had always been easy for William; pretend to stay up late finishing some report for English class and wait a sufficient hour after his parents went to sleep at night. Proceed quietly downstairs. Open door, walk outside. Close door. Continue.

It was unusual, he knew, maybe even dangerous, but there

3

was something about night air, how it brushed your skin in a courteous way and how the street lights seemed like saints on those moonless nights: something calming. It made him remember that there was once a time when one had no worries and the worst pain could only be felt when falling off a bike and hurting your knee. It was a time when happiness was just a hard word to spell, the "i" often being mistaken for a "y," as opposed to something you had to struggle to find, and seventy-five percent of your life was spent outside. This time was called childhood.

Childhood, he thought, reaching the end of the street and sitting casually on the curb, was a time when you didn't know that you didn't know who you were.

"*This is a good spot,*" William thought, tilting his head back and taking in a deep breath of solitude. He was right beneath a street light, flickering with honor as it did every night, William's only companion at a desolate time. It was a good companion, seeing as it never complained, talked rudely or cursed, as many of his friends did. It just stood there and listened, like a guard dog. Or just a lamp.

Reaching into his pockets, music still playing softly, William pulled out a neatly folded sheet of notebook paper, already scribbled on, and a chewed-up pen. He clicked it three times.

William was well liked. He had been on varsity soccer for two years, and the past year he had been named a captain as a sophomore. He was respected among adults and a total hit among his friends, having the capability to still have a good time while sober. No one doubted that he was a generally nice person, and most found it hard to dislike him. He had earned respect on his own, and he was William, the guy who can help you solve your problems. However, there was one thing, he knew, that could change all of that.

William was a poet. Like other myopic teenagers, he commonly found it easier to deal with his emotions by hitting things, especially when he was angry. But it didn't prove to be enough, and it usually ended in a bruised and bloody fist, the result of punching a tree or a brick wall. One winter day, midway through freshman year, a thought occurred to him as he stood outside his house at one in the morning, right hand dripping blood onto the frozen grass: the thoughts that were going through his head were words; words that could be written and read.

*"Weird,"* he thought to himself. *"I didn't think there was such a vivid way to express feelings."* He dug into his pocket, reaching around for anything and finally fishing out a thin, chewed up pen, popping the cap off and grasping it firmly in his shining, crimson right hand. Words came to his head, and the pen met his left arm, putting in ink the thoughts from his head.

That day was the beginning of many things. It was the beginning of his becoming a poet, an aspect of his life that he kept one hundred percent secret, the beginning of his midnight walks around the neighborhood, starting at around once a month and progressing to about two or three times a week. It was also the beginning of a realization that although William had a good life, he was not happy.

Underneath his lamp friend, William wrote, scribbling the words onto his crumpled piece of paper in a precise order that his mind delicately picked out. His poems were a tender balance; put one thing out of place and the rest would topple, so he picked his words with an accuracy that came naturally to him. His poems hardly rhymed. It seemed to him like having a rhyme scheme only put a barrier over what you really had to say, and it was harder to get the true meaning out, so he stuck with free verse, a very loose style of writing.

It was his escape; that which uncorked the bottle that held all his feelings and let them pour out. William wrote at every opportunity he got, keeping himself on the down-low. He knew what people would say if they found him writing poems.

"You write poetry?" Imaginary Friend would say. "Dude, that's hella weird." William wasn't looking for that kind of attention.

The soft crinkling of falling water on the tree leaves brought William out of his writing and back to his quiet reality: rain, the curb, the one-in-the-morning breeze. It was drizzling, and he scrambled to write the last few words before shoving the crumpled paper back in the pocket of his hoodie. As he stood up to leave, his knees cracking a bit, he felt a dead weight in the back of his chest, which seemed to be resisting his difficult endeavor of getting up.

It wasn't uncommon; William very often felt this way, and all that he knew is that it wasn't a good feeling. Not sadness or anger, but more like the lack of happiness, or even the lack of feeling. It started with the weight, and the strange tugging in his chest, and got progressively worse until he could feel a ringing in his ears like a frustrated scream. It frightened him at first, not knowing what he was feeling, but over time William had managed to deal with it, telling himself, "Nothing's really wrong, so I don't need to feel nervous." Still, he couldn't hide the idea from his mind that something wasn't right, and it had been that way for a long time.

William crossed the street parallel to the curb, and meandered slowly down the sidewalk, in no particular hurry to get home, even in the ample rain. He reached out to touch the branches of the neighboring trees gently as he passed, a small collection of rainwater running off each leaf and grazing his hands. William always knew that if they could talk, trees would tell the best stories. They saw everything around them, every event that had happened within their visual range, and heard things that no one was meant to hear. Although they seemed still and sleepy, there was life to them, he knew, and they could make you wonder.

A dark violet cloud pushed its way in front of the half moon, casting dancing shadows on the ground as William walked to the faint beat of the music drifting from his headphones. He passed a small yard, overgrown with weeds and untrimmed grass, one large weeping willow shading the property. It cried with the rain. He looked up suddenly, surprised. A faint sliver of light streamed from the door before it shut quietly, leaving William with one eyebrow raised, stopping to see who had walked out. Or maybe in, he thought.

He stopped and gazed at the secluded house. One generally wouldn't notice it if they didn't take the time to look since it was practically hidden by the unkempt yard around it. It was a small structure, bland color and typical suburban layout with a long driveway and a lawn that desperately needed to be mowed. One window was lit up, somewhere on the second floor. A shadow moved about. Someone was stirring in the room with the light, William noticed, pacing uneasily and then disappearing out of sight. Then the light flickered out. This was Leila's house.

William stood for a few moments, bewildered. He had known that Leila lived here, having seen her walking to and from school, though never receiving more than a friendly 'wussup' head nod or a wave. Like her home, Leila was easy to overlook. She was quiet and hard to spot in school, always slipping away, avoiding eye contact and speaking as minimally as possible. William often wondered about her; why she always carried an old composition book with her, or why she always wore long sleeves, even in the summer. Why she hardly smiled.

What William did know, after half a year of being in the same fifth period art class, was that Leila could draw fairly well; fairly well being a fairly large understatement. Why she never shared any of her work with anyone, not even her closest friends, eluded him. He hadn't sat very close to her, and couldn't see much, though a few times he did remember peeking over her shoulder uninvited, always baffled by what she created.

William had never given Leila as much as a second glance, but now, standing in front of a house that was as quiet and hidden as she was, he couldn't help but think of her, recalling one of the only conversations they had ever really had. It was mid-January, and the temperature in the art room had no significant difference from the weather outside. He walked in, making a desperate attempt to snuggle inside his signature grey hoodie, and noticed Leila sitting alone in the back, looking perfectly at peace with the cold in her simple long sleeved shirt. He walked over and sat beside her, propelled by nothing but curiosity.

"You're not cold?" He asked, plopping himself down clumsily on a stool and tucking his hands inside his pockets, and she looked up for just a moment, before ducking her head back down, wispy curtains of fiery hair falling over her eyes.

"Not really," she muttered, the charcoal in her left hand flying over the sketchbook she had placed in her lap, dancing beauty across the page. William peeked over at the drawing, and instantly raised an eyebrow in awe, leaning in closer for a better look. She didn't shy away. What was on the paper was more than just a face; it was a soul, complete with emotion and thought and depth, more than someone could perceive. It was the face of someone who could spring right out of the portrait and really live.

"Wow," William said. "That's...wow, that's incredible. I mean, I knew you could draw, but this is crazy. That's so good." He saw a sliver of a smile sneak across her lips.

"Thanks," she said, in an almost whispery voice, the sound struggling free.

"Who is it?" William asked, almost immediately. It was a unique face: long, choppy black hair, dark eyes, deep smile lines, true emotion. Leila sat up a little straighter.

"It's this drummer, from a band I really like. He died a few years ago," she answered, eyes cast down while her hand created detail that William didn't even believe had come out of her pencil. Part of his astonishment came from the notion that he had never heard so many words come out of her mouth. He looked at her, almost quizzically, trying to read through her, trying to see into the mind of this budding creative genius, and they locked eyes for a fleeting moment.

"It's amazing. Seriously, you're really talented," he said, trying to coax more words out of her, but getting nothing more than another 'thanks' as she continued to draw. She was like a machine, only offering a few words before she locked herself up again, waiting for the next deposit of five cents. William took another look at the drawing, seeing the downcast face, solemn but full of life. He couldn't help but compare it to Leila herself: quiet, but blooming inside.

Now, in the middle of the night, he gazed at her home, hiding away from the world, from the rain and satisfying emptiness that surrounded him at this desolate time, wondering more and more about the girl that everyone knew, but knew nothing of. William smiled at the thought of her, a crooked half smile, and turned away, continuing his walk back down the path. He always looked down when he walked. Ever since he was young, he walked in step in the sidewalk, always stepping his right foot over the crack before his left. He couldn't remember why, and sometimes worried he'd end up with a face full of cement one day, due to an excess of concentration.

*"Don't be that guy,"* he told himself.

The night whispered. William dragged his feet, trying hard to delay the inevitability of getting home and having to lay awake until sleep crept up at him, gnawing at his ankles and then at his consciousness. He turned onto his street, a dark tunnel with a single lamp post at the far end, its trail of light extended to guide William home. He took its hand. The street looked the way it always did, felt how it always felt, yet there was something out of place, William could feel it, just couldn't tell what it was. It was like solving a puzzle, when you find a piece that looks like it would fit perfectly, but it's slightly wrong, throwing everything off. Something was different; the air smelled sweet and danced around William in a way he had never felt before. It was different and therefore he chose to ignore it.

Creeping up the front steps to the house, William looked over each shoulder once, a habit he had developed after many nights of general hooliganism, each time greeted by the old friendly lamp post with a beaming smile, before opening up the door with the smallest whisper of a sound and stepping delicately inside as if the floor were thin glass. Poking his head outside once more, William inhaled the familiar, yet mysterious night air and turned his back, shutting the door silently behind him.

# TWO

The sun was too bright today, William decided. Pushing through the main double doors of his school, he knew he looked terrible. The translucent skin beneath his eyes was an unnatural shade of stormy blue; tufts of auburn hair stood straight up on his head; he was wearing sweatpants in public. People may have easily mistaken him for a very large, dead bird.

He trudged down the maze of hallways to first period English, acknowledging most people with a nod or a friendly passing-by fist bump. There were blurred spots in his vision, and sound wasn't processing in his mind on time. Anyone else in this sort of half-there, half-not state would think they were sick or dehydrated. To William, it was all normal by now: pounding headaches like stabbing knives, little control of his limbs, a limp mind.

All day, after his first walk that past January, William had begun to think that he was dying or about to pass out, and nearly threw up anytime someone spoke too loud. The first few weeks were disgustingly tiring, but over time, and as the secret midnight meanders became more frequent, it bothered him less and less until it was almost normal for him to act like a zombie.

William pushed through the door of his first period class, a task which required all of his strength, and walked in to a couple of early students sitting on desks or finishing up homework, mustering a few scattered greetings that resonated like alarms going off in his head. Throwing his backpack down and nearly falling into a chair William looked up to find his curly, brunette best friend flouncing toward him, unnaturally energetic at that miserable time of morning.

"Hey, sleepyhead!" she said, smiling in his face as she ruffled his hair.

"Hop off, Emma. I'm tired," William responded, sounding

something like, "gahhhhhh."

Emma made a face and hopped up on his desk, her small figure working to her advantage. "You're always too tired."

Someone across the room yelled, "How could you possibly understand what he just said?" Emma responded with a sharp, derogatory comment.

"I was up doing homework," William lied. "I had a late practice." He pushed Emma off his desk. Although his club soccer team often practiced late, it certainly wasn't the reason for his lack of sleep. Club practice would not even begin for another two months. "Go to sleep." He put his head down. "Bye, best friend."

Emma rolled her eyes and shook her fist at him, the way a crotchety old man might when yelling at a few rotten kids. Nevertheless, she pulled a Marley's Mellow Mood drink out of her bag, took a sip, and walked out of the room to vex somebody else.

The morning passed at an uncomfortably morbid pace, and by fourth period, William had developed a horrible, pulsing headache in his right temple, due in part to the normal high school noise pollution, which seemed to have increased a few decibels. He tried hard to focus on functions and trigonometry, (and how he would never find an appropriate time in his life to insert the use of cosine into an everyday situation), but his mind snuck off, creeping into the dark.

It followed the scratching of pens on paper, to the whisper of secrets from ear to ear, moving swiftly through the popping of gum and past the 'click, click, click' of someone secretly texting behind the back of an oblivious teacher. His mind wandered until it reached a dark, secluded house, overgrown weeds encasing it.

Curiosity opened and secrets closed, tall trees of wonder swayed in the wind of Leila's mystery: her face, her fiery hair, her delicate hands creating. He could feel something crawl around his head.

"Homework, William?"

The house shattered in the dark, and William was back to the present, sitting up straight before his trig teacher, who hovered over him with a red pen in hand, looking unenthusiastic.

"Uh, yeah." William blinked a few times before sliding a crumpled piece of notebook paper to the corner of his desk, complete with a few scribbled answers. His teacher signed sloppy initials across the front of William's half thought-out homework and moved on. William slumped back down in his chair and chewed the clicky end of his pen, his mind blank. Another tantalizing half hour passed; thirty slow minutes of trying too hard to pay attention and instead losing every ounce of focus that he'd had until the bell rang, a little too loud for his fragile, tired state, and he made his way toward the art room, moving sluggishly with the tide of people.

"Hey, Will," a sugar coated voice said, the small figure of a girl sneaking up beside him. She sported skin tight jean shorts, about the same width of a thick belt, a sad, chopped up excuse for a T-shirt, heat damaged straight hair and dark makeup rimmed all around her eyes. She snapped her gum, with a glossed smile. William was repulsed and managed to choke out a "hey," before averting his glace. He wanted nothing to do with the provocative-dressing, drama-summoning females that occasionally said hello to him a little to too sweetly while casually passing by. The girl grinned and turned on her heel, turning heads as well as she walked away.

William felt a light punch on the shoulder and turned to acknowledge one of his varsity teammates, towering over him at six-foot-massive; a junior named Kris, with a K, who had the common sense of a nutmeg jar and somehow managed to stay academically eligible for athletics. His keys were hanging lazily out of his pants pockets. Kris was, in every sense, a tool.

"Dude, was that Cassie?" he asked, swimming alongside Will through the current of people. "Damn, she's hot."

"For real." William raised his eyebrows, only able to nod and pretend to agree, while trying his best not to turn to Kris and say, "You are, in fact, a massive douche." Instead, he replied with, "Yeah, she's cute," a lie that would get Kris off his back. "Later." William thumped him on the shoulder and turned the corner to the art room, opening the door to serenity as he walked in and inhaled the comforting scent of charcoal, oil paint, and fruity air freshener as the high school noise was muted behind him.

The door shut and he lumbered toward the far end of the room, to a few scattered greetings. Leila was sitting at the back table, tapping her pencil against the graffiti covered surface, teeth strangling her bottom lip. She sat by herself, surrounded by papers and charcoal and creative genius; her face wore a blank expression and she sat up straight, white headphone in one ear. As usual, she sported a plain, long sleeved shirt and William couldn't help but wonder how she wasn't theoretically burning up. Her shirt brought out her hair, William noticed: red. When Leila looked up with tired eyes to see William walking toward her, she sank back a little, and attempted to clear a spot for him, nervously shoving everything out of the way, allowing a few papers to flutter to the floor. Her face flushed as he stooped down to pick them up, and she faked a quick smile as he handed them back, sitting down next to her.

He adjusted himself on the uncomfortable art stool, exhaled, and looked over at her with a smile. "Hey," he said. Leila smiled in return for a split second.

"Hi, sorry," she said, quickly. "I've got a lot of...stuff." Disgruntled, she was still shoving papers away into her backpack. "I'm a little disorganized."

William smiled boyishly. "I've noticed," he laughed. She didn't. Clearing his throat awkwardly, he asked, "I can sit here, right? I'm not trying to intrude or anything."

"Oh, yeah." Leila pushed her bangs out of her face. "Go ahead." She was uncomfortable, William noticed. She fidgeted.

Mrs. Davis, the art teacher was known mostly for her striking ability to not give a damn, partially from her lack of professionalism, little respect for dress code, and hipster-like taste in music. This particular day she sauntered into the classroom with her long hair tied up as the second bell rang, looking at each student with a glance of little dignity. She acknowledged the class with a mumble, awkwardly placing her cheap plastic coffee cup on her desk at the side of the room, sitting down slowly on a nearby stool facing the class.

As Mrs. Davis began to ramble about something concerning the finishing touches on self portraits, which no one would even bother to touch, Leila turned to William, gently pushing her golden-red hair aside. It was long, and turned inward toward her face, making her skin glow, somehow making her look more innocent. He couldn't figure out anything of quite the same color.

"Not trying to sound rude or anything, I'm just curious. Why are you sitting here? I mean, due to the fact that you hardly sit here ever," she mumbled, somewhere between a murmur and a whisper. "Do you need something? I have the Spanish homework for Thomas' class if you want it." William could tell she had practiced these words beforehand in her mind. He shook his head, craning toward her while Mrs. Davis droned on.

"I'm just saying hi." He shrugged. "I can leave if you want."

Leila immediately shook her head. "No, no. It's fine." Mrs. Davis looked over for a brief moment, and Leila pasted her lips together, arms crossed.

"Listen while I'm talking," Mrs. Davis croaked, and took a sip of her coffee, continuing to not give a damn. Leila leaned back in.

"I was just wondering." She finished quickly, and sat up straight again.

"I just figured we weren't really...acquainted." William paused, smiling at his big word. "And it would be cool to get to know you. Right?"

Leila nodded. When she smiled, it was with her mouth, not

her eyes. "Yeah," she said. "Yeah, that'd be cool."

The low sonance of Mrs. Davis giving inaudible instructions that no one would follow soon died out and she retreated back to her desk, drowning in the clutter. Amused students got up lazily and meandered about, milling around tables and flocking toward their friends, arms on shoulders, elbows on desks. Amidst the murmur was an audible silence between Leila and William, both shifting uncomfortably in their seats, words caught up in their throats until William slashed the sound barrier again upon seeing Leila reach down and haul a Pre Calculus book onto the table.

"Math? Come on," he teased, an instinctive boyish grin sinking into his skin. "You're the real artist. Shouldn't you be doing something…arty? Slacker." A smile flickered across Leila's downcast face, igniting William's sense of pride.

"Look at Mrs. Davis." Leila snorted. "Does she look like she gives a damn or what?"

*"Another groundbreaking speech from the barren land of Leila,"* William thought to himself, rather impressed. "I know, look." He motioned to the lazy, napping lump of Mrs. Davis, a heap of tired teacher at her desk. "Not dressed professionally at all. So much for respect!" His half smile matched the one that had just snuck across Leila's face.

"So much swag," she said. William chuckled, looking at Leila out of the corner of his eye; she was smiling to herself, pretending to not notice that he was watching, but secretly, he knew, wishing he would. They sat for a minute, in a more comfortable silence, his clear eyes tracing the delicate shape of her face.

A stocky figure had come over to the back table, leaning lazily against the surface. He nodded to Leila. "Sup, Will."

"Hey, man." William acknowledged James, a longtime companion known for his mellow outlook on the world.

"I'm having a bonfire tonight. You should go, Cassie's gonna be there," James said, punching William on his shoulder, the most common of man-hints. "It'll be a good time." He looked at

William with encouraging eyes. William nodded and gave him a signature almost real smile.

"Yeah, I'll have to see if my mom will actually let me out of the house and such. But it sounds cool." Secretly, William was not fond of the idea. As appealing as the bonfire may have sounded, it was one that he did not wish to attend.

"Sweet." James stood up straight again. "Oh, uh, Leila. Do you have the Spanish homework?"

Leila looked up, and before she could nod, or say anything for that matter, William said, "No. She doesn't." When James gave him a quizzical look, he shrank down a bit, saying, "I already asked. She doesn't have it." James shrugged.

"Alrighty. I'll see you later." James walked off, and Leila turned abruptly to William, eyebrows raised. "What?" he asked.

She rolled her eyes. "What was that?"

"What!" William laughed, forcing a smile out of Leila.

"You don't have to do that. There's nothing wrong with 'helping a bro out,'" She said, with the addition of air quotes.

"Oh, so now you're mocking me," William joked. "Well I'm not just about to let him rob you of your hard work." Leila giggled a little at 'hard work.'

"Come on, now. It's Spanish homework," she said, shaking her head at him. "No es muy dificil. I put minimal effort in; I don't mind sharing once in a while. This is high school." Her eyes bore into him. William shrugged.

"Fine. Maybe I won't be so quick to help you out next time."

"Fine!"

"Fine." William turned his back to her, scoffing sarcastically. Out of the corner of his eye, he saw her smiling, though she acted like she wouldn't let him see it. "Hey, can I see the homework for government?" he asked, nonchalantly.

"Shut up."

# THREE

With ten minutes left of sixth period there came an agonizing wait. All attention that had previously gone into learning the correct placement of direct object pronouns in the Spanish context had disappeared within the first half hour, much to the understanding of William's teacher. The warm weather outside beckoned, as did the appealing thought of an after-school nap, and William occupied his time by engaging in a ferocious battle of 'Go Fish' with Emma, who had a tendency to extol her card game slander a little too loudly.

"Seven," Emma declared, fierce blue eyes peering strategically over her impenetrable wall of cards.

"Go fish." William's tired voice showed his lack of enthusiasm, while his eyes drifted lazily toward the immobile clock.

"Damn it!" A few heads turned as Emma angrily dug for a new card, again taking refuge behind her deck.

"Jeez, Emma, shut up a bit," an unsuspected voice echoed from the back of the room.

"Fight me!" Emma said, not turning her head. William asked for a four, nonchalant and bored as his cards bled. "Damn it!" More heads turned in silence as Emma angrily handed over two cards, and frowned as William slapped them onto the desk defiantly, along with the last of his cards.

"Winning," he said. Emma glared.

"New game." Emma began dealing new cards, hands moving fast and ferocious despite her stolid expression, but William didn't notice. His eyes were merely looking, it was his mind that was seeing; seeing Leila's smile and her vibrant personality. He heard her like they were back in the art room, her nervous laugh and her out-of-character speech. He wondered what she thought of him, suddenly concerned, and hoped he didn't sound like too much of a tool. He wondered why she had been wearing long sleeves in seventy degree weather.

"Five," Emma's voice said. William wondered why Leila's parents never mowed their lawn. "Five." How long had she been able to draw so well? "Will!" Emma screeched. Heads turned, and she glared at each one, daring them to make a comment. None did. William snapped his head up, wide eyes looking at Emma expectantly as if he had been paying attention all along, a tiny headache still pulsing by his left temple. "I said, five!"

"Oh." William realized that they were playing Go Fish, and he was holding cards. "I fold." Emma glared at him, lips pursed, before turning around to play with someone else. William felt a prick on his shoulder, and realized someone had poked him carelessly with a pencil for his attention. "What?" he snapped, trance shattered.

"I heard you were talking to Leila today." William recognized the ignorant voice coming from Kris, and felt his stomach tighten, as it often did when he was angry or frustrated. Kris had his phone under his desk and was giving William a look of contempt.

"Yeah. What of it?" William said, half turned away from Kris so he wouldn't see the distasteful expression he wore, wanting very badly to get up and walk away.

Kris shrugged, as if he thought nothing of it, eyes cast down at his phone. "I dunno. I just thought it was a little weird." William stiffened.

"How is that a little weird?" he asked, feeling anger pulse through his veins, trying not to throw his fist right at Kris' face.

"She's a little weird."

"Actually, she's perfectly fine." William's mouth was talking before he gave it consent. "Maybe if you didn't assume things about her, you'd see that." He glared at Kris for a moment, looking as tough as possible but instantly regretting his anger, afraid that Kris may not take it as easily as was expected. Instead, Kris just raised an eyebrow, taking a moment to look up from his phone to stare at William, taken aback.

"Chill, I'm not trying to talk badly about her. Don't get so uptight." He looked at William with a judgemental confusion, and a nervous anxiety settled in William's stomach.

The sound of the bell ripped through the classroom, tearing students from their seats and spilling lively conversation out of their mouths as the weekend formally began. William and Kris locked eyes once more before departing without a word. As William slugged his backpack over his shoulder and headed out the door, Emma caught up with him, punching his shoulder, her frizzy hair bouncing.

"You going to James' bonfire tonight?" she inquired, taking her designated spot next to him as they walked down the teeming hallway. Her energy was nauseating.

"I'll try," William said, keeping his eyes on the floor. "I just have to slip past my parents. It shouldn't be that hard." He almost laughed out loud, thinking about how many times a week he slipped past his parents and how much of a big deal it wasn't. "But yeah, it sounds fun."

"Good. 'Cause James creeps me out." Emma rolled her eyes, preparing for a rant. "Too much weed." William saw her shake her head and her mouth move, but he tuned out the noise, nodding occasionally to act like he was listening. "Oh," she added, and William snapped his head up, upon being addressed directly. "What did you bitch at Kris?" Emma's blue eyes bore into William as he racked his empty mind for an answer. His answer wasn't very adequate.

"Don't worry about it," he said, pushing through the doors into the smoldering glare from the afternoon sun, the heat hitting him like a wall. Emma followed like a nervous dog. There were only a few things she hated more than when William wouldn't tell her every aspect of his life. "What?" he said, upon seeing her troubled expression staring up at him. "It's guy stuff. Sup?" William replied simply, acknowledging a cluster of guy friends as they passed, walking through the crowds of people with Emma trailing him persistently.

"You never tell me anything!" she whined, grabbing the back of his backpack and yanking it annoyingly, a five-foot-four girl in batman All-Stars versus a six-foot, tired boy with an unkempt appearance.

"Calm down, I do so," William grunted, equally as annoyed, pulling Emma off him and putting her back on her designated side where she sighed angrily. "It's just soccer stuff, dude." She gave him a look, saying that she knew that it wasn't just soccer stuff, but she'd let him get away with it anyway.

"Whatever," Emma replied, simply. They walked past the front of the school and a row of busses to the back tennis courts, taking their route home, across the fields behind the school building. "I heard you were talking to Leila though," she said, expressionless, as they made their way through the tall grass, sidestepping bees and butterflies. William shoved her.

"Why is everyone making that such a big deal?" he growled, part joke, part frustration. Emma regained her balance and ran back at William, body-checking him hard.

"So that's what you and Kris were talking about, huh?" she mocked as William picked himself up off the ground, not saying a word. "You wouldn't tell me because it's about a girl! Do you like her? I've never talked to her, I don't think." William glared at her through the foggy barrier in his tired eyes. She grinned.

"No, I don't. I don't understand why it's a big deal," he said, waving to a few friends across the field. "If you grew the balls to finally talk to Alex Manville, would I harass you about it?"

"Excuse me?" Emma screeched. "Yes, you would, but we're not bringing Alex into this!"

William couldn't hold back his own laughter, as he never could when Emma got fired up. "I can talk to him for you," he suggested, raising his eyebrows suggestively. "I hear he's into brunettes." Emma's blue eyes pierced him. Controlling her anger, she simply turned her head to face forward, gripping the straps of her backpack with an unnatural force instead of tackling William as she normally did.

"I do not need you to talk to anyone for me, thanks," she said after about a minute of utilizing her anger coping mechanisms. "I'm perfectly capable of doing it myself." Emma stuck her nose up, defiantly, exactly as William had predicted. He had her distracted.

Summer weather was beginning to peek out from behind a long winter; the sun beat down on William's back and blinded him, the aroma from a nearby honeysuckle bush swimming around his head, fragrant and wholesome. Girls were wearing shorts again and those nice, colorful dresses, and guys were blasting reggae on their iPods, a summertime tradition. Ice cream trucks were already patrolling the streets. Another two months of slacking off until finals, and then came the long days of staying up, sleeping in, and losing track of time.

As they walked home beneath a pastel blue sky dotted with cotton clouds, nothing needed to be said. After years of friendship, silences weren't awkward and no one felt the need to fill them; sometimes it was better when nothing was said. After being accused of being a couple at the beginning of freshman year and after Emma silenced the rumors with her demanding presence, people had grown accustomed to seeing the way they acted around one another: linking arms and insulting each other rather crudely.

"Alright, later, Brosephine," Emma said, William finally noticing that she was heading off her separate way, meandering down a bike path that split the sparse woods in half.

"See you tonight," William called, seeing Emma wave before sticking her ear buds in, walking to her destination with no particular purpose, frizzy hair bouncing around her shoulders, torn-up backpack, Batman converse, 'Recycle, fool' T-shirt and all. William walked past the diverging path, slugging his old trusty headphones on, music flowing into his ears as he made his way home, blocking out the noise of nature and teenagedom, and welcoming the free sound of fast guitar melodies and heavy bass.

Again he floated from his world to another, zoning out and seeing Leila. She was probably walking home as well, not too far from him. How come they had never bumped into each other on their way to school when they lived relatively close? William wondered. Now that he had noticed Leila after his mysterious encounter in front of her house the night before, he couldn't get the questions about her off his mind. He knew she was completely normal; she had her own group of friends, she had dated a football player for half of freshman year, she was talented. She was gorgeous.

William stopped for a moment, standing absolutely still, eyes scanning the woods that had come up ahead of him, the path to his home close by. He had just instinctively admitted to himself that Leila was gorgeous, a thought which would have never occurred to him if he hadn't sat next to her today. He walked on again, focusing on his surroundings. He wouldn't have sat next to Leila today if he hadn't seen her light on last night, and he wouldn't have seen her light on last night if he hadn't been meandering around the neighborhood at two in the morning. This thinking was digging deep into his mind, causing the pulsing headache to return, yet he couldn't get his mind off of her. What was it that made her so reserved?

He walked down the path, crossing a familiar wooden bridge which he crossed nearly every day, under which a creek had run dry. It was a picturesque scene, with all the greenery surrounding him in different shades, the trunks of the trees digging deep and strong into the ground. If only the water had been running.

Coming off the path and stepping into the familiar territory of his backyard, he was greeted by an annoying chorus of barks as his two dogs, Damian and Squeakers, pawed at the sliding glass door, too excited for their own good. William rolled his eyes and walked around the side of the house, weaving in and out of the numerous, thriving bushes that occupied his mom's garden. Climbing up the porch steps with the last of his energy, William fished in his pocket for his keys, fumbling with them for a moment before unlocking the door and pushing it open, more with his body than his hands.

"Hi, honey!" A boring falsetto rang from the living room.

"Hi, Mom." William trudged from the little foyer up the stairs, depositing his backpack in its designated spot on the floor to see his mom lying on the couch with a cup of tea beside her, reading.

"How was school?" she asked, not looking up from her book.

"Are you going back to work today?" William ignored her question, shuffling into the kitchen and opening the fridge intuitively, jumbling a few things around until he found a clear bottle of organic apple juice, one-hundred percent natural. He held it up. The liquid rolled off the glass with a cleansing rumble.

"No." His mother's voice floated in from the other room. "How was school?"

"Why not?" He asked between gulps of cool juice.

"How was school, bubbule?"

"Fine," William choked out, still haunted by the Yiddish nickname that his mother had used for him all his life. He opened the cabinet and grabbed himself a bag of pretzels before sliding out of the kitchen where he couldn't be asked any more questions. Down the hall, he opened the door to his bedroom, uncomfortably bright light filling the small space as he flopped himself down on his bed, sighing heavily with the content of finally being able to rest.

His phone vibrated as he began to close his eyes. *"I'm just imagining it,"* William thought, desperately. *"No one's really texting me."* Nevertheless, three agonizing vibrations rippled through his pocket and he angrily tore his eyes open, pulling his phone out with a little too much force. The number was not recognized.

"Hey, Will," it read, with a little beaming smiley face. "It's Cassie. I was wondering if you were going to James' bonfire?" William chucked himself back on his pillow, not wanting to write back.

"Hey, Cassie. It's Will," he typed, mocking her slightly. "Um, I'm trying to go, yeah. You?" Frankly, William thought, he didn't care if Cassie went. He wasn't interested. If his friends thought that dressing provocatively and wearing too much makeup was attractive, they could express their own interests in that.

"William?" his mother's voice suddenly echoed from somewhere down the hall. "Are you going to be home for dinner?" William winced, pulling his pillow over his face like he could drown in it.

"Um, I was thinking of going out," he answered, as painlessly as he could, the words blurting themselves out. Sprawled out uselessly in his bed, he winced in preparation for whatever words he might hear. William braced himself, and instead found only a tangible silence. "Mom?"

He heard an audible sigh from the living room.

"Honey, it's Shabbat." William squeezed his eyes shut, trying to make the words go away. If only the Sabbath fell on a Thursday.

"I was gonna go to James'," he called softly, mustering sensitivity to his voice. "He's having a bonfire. Just a few people." William knew that was a lie but he kept talking, his nervous attempt to fill his mother's silence.

"I'm getting a ride with Emma. I'll be home around eleven or twelve." He couldn't see her, but he knew his mom would be laying her head back on the couch, lifting her book back up to her eyes, so used to the situation that she had no particular feelings.

William slammed his pillow over his face, already playing the scene in his head. Instead of two tall candles illuminating the center of the table, with William and his parents blessing the bread and the wine in their limited Hebrew, there would only be an empty chair and a space to fill. Meaningless chatter, not prayer. He almost wanted to stay home tonight, eat dinner with his parents and not worry about party drama. He wanted to stay up until two in the morning playing *Call of Duty*, and pass out on the couch. He wanted to remind himself that he was Jewish.

Instead, he was unofficially obligated to a few teenagers to go to some teenager party where he was forced to do teenager-like things and have a mediocre time. For a moment, pillow-faced William considered calling Emma, telling her he couldn't make it that night; he was sick or his parents grounded him or something like that. His hand gripped his phone and lingered there for a moment, until he forced his fingers from their clutching.

# FOUR

"Wilfred, get in the car!" Emma, using an old nickname, called from her brother's old minivan, her head poking through the shotgun window while the noise from the car radio managed to pierce William's eardrums. It was a quarter to seven, and William forced himself from his pleasant nap, shoved his phone and a few dollars into his pockets and headed for the door, walking awkwardly past his parents making dinner together.

"I'm leaving," he told them, the smell of onions and chives frying in the kitchen making him slightly dizzy.

"Alright, have fun," his dad said, not looking up from the bread he was slicing. "Keep your phone on. Be back before twelve."

"I will," William answered automatically, hurrying down the stairs and out of the house, shutting the door quietly behind him. He crossed the front lawn, decorated with yellow and purple wildflowers, a protective layer of tree branches overhead, to where Emma and her older brother, Randy, had parked rather crudely, Dan the Big Blue Van humming with the distaste of having to demonstrate any sort of movement. The side door was already open and waiting for him.

"Howdy," Randy greeted William as he jumped in the van, pushing assorted junk to the side for room.

"Hey!" he said, shutting the door and patting Emma on the head, their usual greeting. "What's cracking, Randy?" Dan the Van grumbled a little before pulling away from William's house and chugging down the street with what little dignity he had.

"Not much, little bro," Randy said, blasting his dubstep from the car's speakers. Emma started up a headbang, her curly hair flying. William snickered, grabbing a strand of hair and pulling it slightly and watching it snap back into place, causing Emma to shriek and smack him across the head.

"Decided where you're going to college yet?" He asked, ignoring the gruesome faces that Emma was making at him from the front seat. Emma's older sister, Stacey, was already in her third year at the University of Maryland, and Randy was up next, about to graduate with a 4.0, just as Stacey had. Emma had a long way to go.

A grin spread involuntarily across Randy's sunburned face, though he didn't try to hold it back. "Funny story, actually." He made a sharp turn, causing the assorted piles of junk that occupied Dan the Van to shift uncomfortably. "It appears that I got a full scholarship to Penn State. So, I suppose I'll be going there."

"Dude!" William's smile exploded. "Dude! Congrats, man. That's literally awesome. How are you not freaking out?"

Randy laughed, a ringing, musical sound. "I am. I just don't show it. I'm actually psyched."

"Cool!" Emma interrupted with a goofy tone of voice. "You go to an amazing college for free and have a great college time while I'm stuck in high school for two more years." She pursed her lips and glared at the two of them staring blankly back at her, while Dan the Van chugged on.

"Get good grades," Randy said simply, turning onto a narrow residential street. As Emma rolled down the windows, a heavy mist of voices and party sounds came drifting in, and William had to suppress a sigh as a familiar song with a bad beat played nearby, drowning in whiney, auto-tuned voices. The world no longer appreciated good music.

"Here we are, munchkins," Randy said, parking Dan the Van by the curb of a boring, well maintained home flooded with the noise of James' bonfire. "Have a fun time. Don't do drugs, don't talk to strangers. Text me when you need a ride home. Get outta my car." He smiled, a familiar scar on his cheek defining his face.

"Thanks, Randy," William said, hopping out of the car after Emma and giving a halfhearted wave as Dan the Van chugged his way down the road. The two walked awkwardly across the lawn to the back of the house, where they found a typical teenage party, with a few typical teenagers sitting around a typical bonfire, waving at Emma and William with goofy smiles. A few were playing an intense game of volleyball, while most were just sitting around, cuddling, or roasting various foods. The bad music pulsed.

"Sup, guys," Emma said first, hopping right down in the circle around the fire, which was already blazing, smoke rising to the gradient sky. William smiled and gave a friendly wave as he was greeted with a chorus of 'hellos' but stood hesitantly beside the group, offering some handshakes to assorted acquaintances.

"Bro!" James called, walking off the makeshift volleyball court with a huge grin. "And, bro-ette. Glad you could make it," he said excitedly, clapping William on the shoulder.

"Yeah, same," William said, which was the second thing to come to his mind. The first was the fact that he was missing Shabbat dinner for this.

"Hey," James leaned in a little closer, the overwhelming scent of Axe body spray flooding William's senses. "I think Cassie was looking for you. You should go talk to her." He smiled and gestured to where Cassie was sitting, wearing a shirt that wasn't really big enough to qualify as a shirt and more dark makeup than William thought was humanly possible. He thought, for a moment, that she had been punched in both eyes.

"Yeah," William said, both hesitantly and truthfully. "Yeah, I will." He looked down at his sweatpants, a little disappointed in his own fashion sense, and walked slowly over to where Cassie was sitting, feeling nervous yet still slightly repulsed. He could smell her perfume from a few feet away. Emma gave him a curious look, which he ignored with dignity, sitting down beside Cassie as if it was nothing.

"Hey," he said.

Cassie turned and smiled up at him, her lips looking shinier than a bald man's head. "Hey," she replied, dragging the word out and flicking her long, hair behind her bare shoulders. Her skin glowed. "Glad you could make it."

William smiled, smoothing down a few tufts of hair that stood vertical on his head. "Wouldn't miss it," he lied, nervous guilt filling his stomach.

"Nice sweats." The corners of Cassie's mouth twitched upward, and William felt his face flush slightly as a laugh trickled out of her.

"Well," he started, racking his brain for a response. "Long day." It sounded questionable, like he was looking for approval rather than stating a fact. Cassie laughed, pulling one of her knees up to her chest. Around them, more assorted figures approached the bonfire, abandoning their volleyball game and plopping one by one into the grass, picking up abandoned conversations. Someone cranked the music up, bass pounding the earth.

"Will!" someone, a junior named Sean called, sitting cross-legged beside a few friends. "Are you going to get it in, or what?" He laughed loudly and William felt a little twitch inside him. A few people looked over, eyebrows raised, and Cassie made a small scoffing noise, though she eyed him curiously as he racked his brain for a witty comeback. Emma, as usual, was one step ahead of him.

"Your douchebaggery is not appreciated," she said casually, shooting Sean a threatening glance, coated with cuteness. "Please take your remarks elsewhere and leave my best friend alone." A few hearty laughs accompanied the high fives that Emma received, but Cassie only looked at him disappointed.

"Are you and Emma, like, a thing?" she asked with a sour expression. "I mean, it's weird you guys are pretty best friends."

"What?" William felt a ripple swim down his spine. He stared at Cassie almost angrily. "Dude, that's like, incest." He shook his head. "No. She's my best friend. Is that not allowed or something?" Cassie stared at him for a minute, mouth open slightly in confusion before she sighed and turned away.

"Whatever," William watched with a slight disappointment as Cassie stood up and walked off, a few heads turning in her direction, but he didn't dwell on it. She was pretty, he had no shame in admitting it, but he preferred talking to people with a real personality, he decided. Some didn't, he noted, as Cassie walked over to a small group of guys and started up conversation, having no problem connecting with their eagerness to be around her.

Receiving various disappointed looks from Emma, Sean and James, William could only shrug and sit back, feeling slightly relieved as Cassie stared back at him every few seconds, obvious disdain in her pale blue eyes. James sat down next to William, breathing in the fresh night air with deep inhalations and nodding his greeting.

"Dude," he said. "That was silly of you."

William could only shrug and sigh deeply. "Well, she isn't really my type," he admitted, to which James made a face. "I'm just here to hang." He leaned back, reclining on his elbows, the dewy grass tickling his skin.

"Alright, I got you," James said. "But there's always the option of 'truth or dare,' you know." He elbowed William in the ribs.

"We'll see." William smiled.

*  *  *

Around eleven-thirty, William silently pushed the front door open, a skill which had been perfected over the last year. He took the key out of the lock and throwing it in his pocket, turned back to the street and waved to Randy and Emma before Dan the Van chugged off into the distance. The only light came from the dim kitchen. William shut the door without a sound and threw his shoes in the corner of the small landing, ascending the stairs to be greeted by Squeakers, anxiously wagging his tail, his tongue lolling out of his mouth as he almost smiled up at William. Damian, the slightly less intelligent one, was certainly fast asleep in his bed.

"Hi, buddy," William greeted Squeakers with a whisper, scratching the Burmese Mountain Dog behind his ears, being rewarded with a film of black hair left behind on his hand. The smell of dog wasn't quite as overwhelming as the smell of Cassie's perfume, which still lingered. William crept down the hallway and into his room, flicking the light on, giving his drooping eyelids a little jolt. Damian lay at the foot of his bed, taking up as much room as a two-year-old corgi could, his legs twitching slightly as he dreamed.

His room was as clean as ever, although his definition of clean would differ from others, being that things were all over the place, yet he could still spot his floor and other objects of significance. This was a noteworthy accomplishment. Pushing a few things aside he muddled his way across the room, shoving Damian out of the way a bit before he dropped down on his bed, swarming with the familiarity of a mattress used for years.

His body was tired, but his mind was buzzing with sharp thought current. Half of his brain was scolding him.

"Way to go, Will," it told him, sarcastically. "That was a tool move. You don't even like Cassie." William shoved the reasonable side of him aside and welcomed the compliments of his other, rambunctious conscience.

"Nice one, bro," it said, giving him an imaginary high-five. "You're quite the ladies' man."

Conscience one rolled its eyes. "It was one girl. He doesn't even like her."

"So?" The other half of his mind said, annoyed. "She's cute. Might as well seize the opportunity while it's right in front of you."

His good conscience theoretically punched his bad conscience in the mouth, and both were silent. William rolled into a deep, much-deserved rest.

# FIVE

Out of nowhere, William awoke. He hadn't been dreaming and the house was silent, his alarm clock beaming blue. 3:14 a.m. Squinting, William rolled over begrudgingly and picked his phone up off the floor, yet there were no new messages or calls. Damian was still asleep beside him. He sat up a little, fighting the nagging sleeplessness that crawled around him and scratched his head, wondering why he was awake. Outside his window, a street light glowed.

He had seen that same light flicker in the dark enough times to know it better than he knew himself, looking to it for familiarity every night before he fell asleep. William almost disregarded it before turning his attention away, but something caught his eye at the last minute, and he snapped his head back for another glance. Someone was standing beneath it.

At first, all William could think was, "Who would go for a walk at 3:14 in the morning?" Then he remembered, "Oh, yeah. I would." He got up carefully, trying not to disturb Damian, and trod across the floor to the window at the opposite wall, still in his clothes from the day before. Glancing past his own reflection in the glass, he saw a female figure, about five-foot-five, standing below the light, wearing oversized grey sweatpants and a black shirt. Her red hair was tied up except for her bangs, which veiled her face delicately like fragile flames, blowing around porcelain skin stained with knowledge.

"What the heck, Leila," William muttered, making his way out the door, whispering through the hallway, down the stairs and out of the house as he always did, but with more urgency this time. He shut the door without a sound, jogging senselessly across the front yard and across the street, wondering what he was even doing. Leila turned and jumped back, seeing William charging over, looking sleep deprived and somewhat insane, raising an eyebrow as he stopped short in front of her. There was a pause, and silence.

"Uh," he said. "Hi." He ran a hand over his head, trying to flatten the hair that had flown up, cowering slightly from Leila's inquiring glance. She folded her arms silently, long sleeves pulled tight over her hands, looking up at him, perplexed. Deep brown eyes gazed into his. "What are you doing?"

Leila made it clear that she was trying not to be surprised, although William knew she couldn't deny that it would be weird for anyone to see anyone else taking a walk at three in the morning. "Nothing," she said simply, looking at him with an unabashed confidence that William had never seen before. "How about you?" There was obvious sarcasm in her voice though her gentle eyebrows furrowed in confusion. The pauses between her words split the air like sabers.

William gazed at her light. She illuminated the dark air around them, shining brighter than the saint-like lampposts, fiery red hair blowing with the warm breaths of wind. She had all the beauty of nature in her.

"Um…" William hesitated, glancing down the street once before turning back to her, searching the confines of his tired mind for an answer, only to be pulled into a decadent trance by her face; one part amused, two parts astonished. "I don't know," he surrendered. "I just saw you outside and kind of freaked out. You probably shouldn't be out this late. Or, uh, early." William winced upon hearing his own words.

Leila muffled a snort, though in a gentle way. "And what were *you* doing up this late, sir?" she asked, a daring half-smile digging into her skin. William flushed.

"I was just…up late," he admitted, shrugging slightly. He wanted to say something to her about the dangers of wandering around so late at night, or early in the morning, but the white headphones around her neck caught his eye, and curiosity bound him tightly. "What are you listening to?" he asked, before he could control himself.

Leila drew the headphones from around her neck and handed them to William, who took them hesitantly, awkward air still flowing around him. "Some progressive stuff," she said, and William's mind sparked. Progressive music was a rather astonishing preference for Leila, it seemed to him, though with her artistic literacy, anything seemed possible. He put the headphones over his head and heard a familiar song playing by a band he knew very well.

"Dream Theater, huh?" William asked, giving her a smile. "Smart girl. You've got good taste." He listened for a minute, drowning out the ambiance of nighttime silence before returning the headphones to Leila, who took them gracefully. Her body flowed like water; quiet but with underlying influence.

"I'm honored," she said, with a smirk, though her eyes were thanking him. "Thanks. I like music. It was sort of forced upon me at a young age." Leaning back against the street lamp, Leila showed the first signs of fatigue, her eyes welling with exhaustion. "I guess you'd think that would make me hate it. But I don't."

Silence ensued, interrupted only by the quiet acapella music of surrounding cicadas and the harmonious rustle of leaves against leaves shaken by the breeze.

"I should walk you home," William stated, dumbly staring at Leila as she stared at her shoes. She glanced up at him through her eyelashes, causing his gut to kick into gear, flipping in spastic circles. He felt funny, frankly.

"Okay," she said, her voice as peaceful as autumn. "If you want. Thanks."

They walked in silent unison, William to the outside of the path that ran parallel to the road and Leila with her delicate movements, walking, hidden by shyness, as William's eyes glanced at her frequently, always falling upon the brown eyes and glowing energy and, most significantly, her beauty. Hidden in sweatpants and the shadows of the nighttime, she was still bright with energy and wisdom.

They turned a corner onto Leila's street and walked slowly to the end of her driveway, William staring up at the small house, concealed with branches and secrets.

"Thanks, Will," she said, facing him slightly, though gazing down the street, as if searching for far-off headlights. She brushed crimson hair out of her face.

"Sure," William said. He buried his hands in his pockets. "Just... try not to sneak out and stuff. It's bad."

Leila laughed faintly. "Yeah, you too." She looked at him knowingly. William froze, embarrassed, but tried to push the thought out of his mind. Did she know he had been walking before? "You won't tell anyone about this, right?" she asked, not pleading but inquiring, hoping she could trust a vague friend.

William nodded. "No, of course not," he said. The thought hadn't even occurred to him to begin with, but he could understand her concern. If anyone caught him taking walks at three in the morning, an activity most would frown upon, he would prefer it was kept a secret. "I got you," he added, sparking a grin.

"Thanks," she said again. Without another word she walked up the front steps and into the house, bringing Williams silence to shame. He stood and watched her disappear suddenly, wondering why she hadn't been nervous or flipped a bitch-fit on him. Any other girl would have been freaked out, he figured, but Leila remained eerily calm for someone with an apparent lack of confidence. She hadn't called him out for spying or sneaking around or anything, just asked what he was doing. It was unusual.

William turned and walked back toward his street, making a straight line down the middle of the road just because he could, burying his hands in his pockets. He sighed, exhaling what felt like about half of his body weight and looked up at the sky, a few glimmering specks visible between the fingers of the overlying trees. He wondered how far away they were, and how long it would take to walk there.

Only a few million years, he figured. Maybe someone had written a book about it, walking to the stars. It would make an epic journey. Maybe *he* would write a book about it, someday.

Then, for a moment, William was blinded. Headlights, like two gleaming eyes peeked out across the wide stretch of road ahead of him, a few hundred feet away, as a small car raced toward him in the darkness. The lights grew brighter and William sprung to life, leaping out of the road and behind the closest tangible thing large enough to conceal him, which happened to be a bush. Hidden in an instant, William crouched, breathing heavily as the headlights grew and the car rushed past him, disappearing down the dark road.

It happened sometimes, though rarely, that a car might pass down the street when William was walking. He would freeze, hide, and imagine every horrible scenario of getting caught by the cops, a friend, or his parents. The car would pass and he would step back onto the road, the smooth asphalt terrain extending like part of his soul, and continue nonetheless.

The light vanished as the machine disappeared down the vacant street, chugging relentlessly into the night, and William made his way back into the road, frazzled but proceeding as normal.

An hour later he lay in his bed again, thinking about nothing but Leila and the nighttime.

# SIX

At around nine-thirty that Saturday morning, William thought he heard a voice. He looked at the clock, lifting his resistant eyelids with a bit of struggle.

"Nahh," he thought to himself. "It's nine-thirty on a Saturday morning. I don't think I'm getting up." Promptly throwing his head back onto the pillow, William fell back into an easy sleep.

Only minutes later, the voice returned, itching his ears as he yanked his eyes open.

"William, time to get up," his mom called from the kitchen.

"Tuhhhh." William tried to block the voice out, rolling over on his side with a slight grunt, fighting to keep his eyelids from closing. It was nine-thirty. And he was *not* getting up at nine-thirty on a Saturday.

The voice disappeared momentarily and William allowed his eyes to close for just an instant, but soon enough light footsteps could be heard plodding down the hallway, growing closer and closer until he heard his door creak open and felt the presence of his mother standing over him. He scrunched his face up, trying to block out the morning. Light was already pouring though his half-closed curtains, showering his unkempt room in golden light. It was painfully blinding.

"Come on, Will." Her voice, soothing but firm, blasted through his slumber. "Get up. You're wasting the whole day."

He grumbled something muffled, head stuffed into his pillow. He heard his mom pick a few clothes off the floor and toss them into the hamper easily, routinely. William would occasionally imagine her as some famous basketball player, sprinting across the court with dirty laundry and dunking it straight in the basket, hanging victoriously from the rim as the crowd of mothers around her went wild. Of course, his mom was only five-foot-one and would probably need a step ladder to reach the net, but she handled his floor-ridden laundry like a pro.

Maybe, William thought, she would go away if he wished hard enough. He would imagine her walking out of his room and back down the hallway; the light would diminish from his room and he would fall back asleep in an instant. Then again, maybe he could find himself an ocean dwelling porpoise to carry him to Madagascar, where he would spend his life fishing and photographing mountains for a postcard company. Neither, he realized, were likely to happen anytime soon.

"Get up." He felt the blanket fly off him and land on the floor with a soft thump. "It's already nine-thirty."

"It's *only* nine-thirty," William grumbled, pushing his limp body up to a sitting position as his mother, crowned with a smile of victory, sauntered out of his room. Making his way down the hallway to his bathroom, William heard gentle voices, *Morning Edition* on National Public Radio coming from the kitchen. It seemed like such an essential part of his household; he woke up to *The Writer's Almanac* with Garrison Keillor, and came home to *Tell Me More*. It was like he knew the hosts on a personal level, hearing these radio shows so often. He was in his element.

Upon turning on the light in the bathroom, William jumped at his reflection in the mirror. His eyes were red and the skin beneath them was almost transparent, dark and thin. Half of his hair stood straight up while the other half lay flat on his head, sticking out in every direction. Dull skin, dull mind. His body lagged as he turned the shower on, waiting a few seconds before getting in and letting the pounding water wake him naturally. The warmth expanded across his skin in a fluid motion, setting his blood flowing, bringing his senses back to life.

Once he was showered and adorned with a new pair of sweatpants, William grabbed a poppy seed bagel from the freezer and sat, watching for four and a half minutes as it toasted. He wondered if he would spend the rest of his life taking walks at night and waiting for bagels to cook. Will made his way back into his room, planning on spending the rest of the day doing anything that included his bed and food.

Damian had been lying on his bed lazily, his tongue hanging out and legs twitching in the midst of a dream, but he perked up instantly when William walked in with his bagel, bounding off the bed and landing with an ear-shattering thud on the carpet.

"No, Damian," William said, taking a seat on his bed and burying himself in the covers again. Damian placed his head in William's lap, a bit too forcefully, giant eyes staring up, hoping to obtain some food. "And stop staring into my soul." He bit into his bagel, and Damian grunted a little, as if to say, *"Shut up, Will. I don't need your sass."*

He reached for a book on the table beside his bed, finding *The Two Towers* and opening to a random page, something he generally did when re-reading a book. He had first read Tolkien's trilogy as a child, though at the time he wasn't quite old enough to understand the overwhelming power and big words. However, he was so drawn to them, the characters and a surreal, fantasy world and all the fighting and nasty stuff, that he read the books again. And again. And grew up with them until he himself seeped into the pages and became part of the story, inhaling more knowledge with each read.

It was silly, he understood, but a part of him was always hoping that one day some archeologist would dig up the ruins of Middle-earth or find *some* leading proof that not all of it was fiction. He spent his life believing that it wasn't only a myth, but a history, a resonance of something past. Something of such depth and power, he believed, couldn't have been made up or dreamt. It was something he didn't plan on ever mentioning out loud.

William was lost in paper, his mind in some distant world while his body was still curled up in bed, reading. An hour passed, and he moved only to breathe, sneeze a few times and take a bite of his bagel. Another hour and his phone interrupted his conscious dream, the ugly buzzing noise penetrating his thoughts. Looking up, annoyed, William found a slightly overcast sky outside his window and a gleaming cell phone beside his bed.

Two new messages. He opened the first one.

*"Hey."* From Cassie. William ignored it, immediately opening the next one.

*"Hang?"* From Emma.

Reluctantly, William closed his book and placed it on the floor beside his bed, rising up delicately and padding across his room, yawning. With stiff, almost robotic motions, he reached into an already open dresser drawer, and pulled out a grey T-shirt with sick yellow letters. "Hawthorne River High School," it read.

*"Formally known as hell,"* William thought. He sprayed little Axe, grabbed his keys from the floor and left his room. "Mom?" he called. "I'm going to Emma's."

"When are you coming home?" she called back.

"I don't know. Today." William left the house and started down the path to Emma's house, a route he could walk blindfolded or in the dark or backwards, on his hands if he felt the need. He passed two small playgrounds and a few wooden bridges, stable over flowing creeks. Mid-sized houses of the same layout and a man jogging. He was no longer satisfied with this provincial neighborhood and he had known it for a while.

It had been a nice place to grow up, but it was somewhat like clothing; you either grew out of it or grew tired of it, and William was certainly grown out of it, unable to be bound by the suburban town's limits. There was a world away from similarly structured homes and neighborhood pools, something more promising calling to him.

He wanted a bustling city: bright lights, energy and a purpose, not just a place. He wanted to get into Georgetown, live in Washington, and travel the unexplored beauty of the world. Maybe intern at the Library of Congress and hide in the endless foundation of words. He wanted to live unconditionally.

For now, he would live limited, walking at night and writing in secret, getting a decent GPA in school and hanging out, like teenagers did. He would obey his parents for as long as he got the opportunity, and disobey them whenever he didn't. He would live limited for now.

Randy, who was just pulling out of the driveway as William walked up Emma's front steps, gave a brisk wave and sped off the street, Dan the Van complaining to no avail. William knocked once before letting himself in.

"Hey, guys!" he called, closing the door behind him and walking upstairs, where Emma's dad reclined on the couch, a guitar under his arm. Folk music hummed quietly in the background. "Hey, Mr. Avery."

"Hey there, Will. How you doing?" Mr. Avery smiled, warm and friendly, playing a C chord. Emma walked into the living room, dressed down in a cut-off shirt, long hair tied up, no makeup. She held a ukulele in one hand.

"Hey, man," she said, as she bit into an apple. "Padre?"

"Yes?" Mr. Avery answered.

"We're out."

Another C chord played in response, and William followed Emma back outside, jumping down the front steps to be greeted by pleasant spring weather. Scents of suburbia overwhelmed him: honeysuckle and mulch and heat. Rays of sun drowned the street in gold; the basketball hoop and the street hockey goal in front of it, lying on its side. A lawnmower chugged.

"What have you been up to, young man?" Emma asked, tossing her apple core into the yard as she took her spot to William's left, striking up "Somewhere Over the Rainbow" on her ukulele. "Besides, you know, making out with Cassie. Good lord." She rolled her eyes, snickering.

William sighed, shoving Emma to the side. "Hey, shut up about it. It's just a one-time thing." His face was already red with embarrassment.

"Liar!" Emma laughed. "You looooove her. I don't really approve actually, but whatever makes you happy, bro."

"I don't!" William cried. "Jeez, Emma. Get it through that goofy head of yours. We just hooked up; I'm not trying to start anything." Emma did not seem to have heard him and struck up the tune again, altering the lyrics slightly.

"Will...is...so in love with Cassie," she sang. "He wants...to have...her babies. Wait." William glared at her, exasperated. "That didn't make sense." Emma corrected herself. "Unless she has some form of male genitalia."

"Emma!" William snatched the ukulele out of her hands and held it above his head. "Shut up. I don't need your sass." Emma jumped in earnest frustration, the ukulele just out of her reach, until she finally leapt high enough and grasped the side, pulling it back down in her arms. Still, she was grinning.

"Alright, alright, fine. You don't like her." There was a pause. "You're just a cheap man slut who hooks up with girls at random." She punched him hard in the arm.

"Gah. I swear, Emma. One of these days..." But William couldn't hide the smile on his face. "What about Alex, huh? Do I harass you about Alex?"

Emma pursed her lips, flicking the strings of her ukulele. "Yes you do, William Jacob Spencer. You harass me every day." She stopped short, striking a confident pose: one hand on her hip the other flipped outward, like she was showing off a new diamond ring. "Oh my gosh, Emma," she said, in a sour, mocking voice. "Grow some balls and talk to Alex Manville. He's totally hot."

"Oh please." William shoved her along. "Let's get food."

Along with a lonely grocery store, a community bank, a Walgreens and a dismal high school, Pitt's Pizza was one of the only mildly satisfying attractions that the Hawthorne River neighborhood had to offer. After a high priced, yet poor quality hair salon went out of business, the building stood unoccupied for almost two years until mysterious trucks began to park out in front of it. Boxes were unloaded and soon enough Pitt's Pizza opened just three months later.

It was the neighborhood place of rendezvous. You needed a place to meet up with your friends? Pitt's. A place to study away from home? Pitt's. Somewhere to watch the news when your TV was broken? Pitt's had you covered. It was a cozy place, with a few small tables in the center and plush couches toward the far wall, an elaborate bookcase on one side and a cooler on the other, holding an everlasting supply of Marley's Mellow Mood iced teas. Their pizza was delectable and cheap, and their employees were good friends of just about everyone.

It was only a ten-or-so minute walk to Pitt's, and a scenic route at its finest amidst a true Maryland spring. They walked leisurely along the side of the road, talking loudly and waving to cars that passed by, singing along to Emma's ukulele.

The sleigh bells on the door jingled as they entered Pitt's, feeling easy and comfortable in the familiar atmosphere laced with the scent of wholesome, delicious pizza grease. It was fairly empty, aside from one woman waiting beside the counter, Blackberry in one hand.

"Hey, man." Emma waved to Jeremiah, who stood behind the register, looking anything but attentive. She walked over, starting up some conversation. William snaked past an array of tables to one of the coolers, grabbing two bottles of Mountain Dew and stopping to stare at the bookcase; or, rather, lack of bookcase.

"Dude. Where's the bookcase?" he asked, walking up to the register and placing the two bottles on the countertop. "This is blasphemy."

Jeremiah punched a few keys. "My boss took it out yesterday," he said, solemnly. "He said it was taking up too much space. I don't know. I kind of liked it." He collected William's crumpled two dollars and handed back ten cents.

"What an abomination," William muttered. "Taking away books."

"For shame," Emma agreed, not really concerned. "I got you a bagel."

"I already had a bagel this morning."

"Well, have another one," Emma said, taking a Mountain Dew off the counter. Jeremiah handed William a freshly toasted bagel on a paper plate.

"It's because I'm Jewish, isn't it," William said, but he smiled and took a bite.

"Yes," Jeremiah and Emma answered. The lady waiting beside the counter looked up from her Blackberry to raise a suspecting eyebrow. Waving goodbye to Jeremiah, William and Emma walked outside into the morning.

"What a tremendous day," Emma said, light breezes rippling through her hair.

"It's too hot." William replied. "What do you wanna do?" He started walking across the parking lot, turning onto Hawthorne River's main road.

"Well first," Emma started, "you have to tell me about this Cassie situation." William rolled his eyes. "Did you hook up with her, or something?" she mocked.

Groaning, William only walked on. "Do we have to talk about this?" he asked, munching his bagel angrily. "Let a Jew be, I'm eating my damn bagel."

"Of course we do. What kind of question is that?" she scoffed, sipping her Mountain Dew. "I'm drinking a damn soda. We can still talk. Do you like her?"

"No."

"What?" Emma's voice rose to a decibel that would deafen a large truck. "You can't just hook up with her and expect that to be it. You manwhore!" William, slightly taken aback, raised a condescending eyebrow. "No. That's not okay. Why would you do that?"

"I...the opportunity came up." William stammered, not used to being criticized so harshly. "She wasn't disappointed, or anything. She *wanted* to." Emma stopped walking, crossing her arms in frustration, her facial expression stone cold.

"You know, she's only going to want more," she said, staring at him harshly. "Even if you're not hurting her, you're going to end up hurting yourself. It's not like she's going to leave you like that. She's unsatisfied." William could only roll his eyes. "You've given her a totally superficial impression of you," Emma went on. "It's going to be a bigger issue than you think it is, trust me."

William put his hands up in surrender. "Alright, alright. I was wrong, and I'm a manwhore. I screwed up and won't do it again, okay? There's no need to be so cold."

"Sorry," Emma mumbled. "It just came out."

William rolled his eyes, but with less insult than before, and put a friendly arm around Emma's shoulder. "Let's go to the pond."

# SEVEN

Hawthorne River was a plain neighborhood, lacking pizzazz, but certainly not lacking beauty. There was a pond hidden beneath a canopy of trees in the woods behind Pitt's which hoarded many different people with different purposes. In the morning it was buzzing with small children, who gave way about midday to people like William and Emma, who made it their favorite, personalized spot. Later on in the afternoon it was generally inhabited by older folks, middle aged parents taking walks or an afternoon jog, and older couples relaxing together. Later in the night, it was overwhelmed with hooligans.

William and Emma walked a short distance down the bike path to the pond, which sat utterly still in the warmth of the sun and the shelter of the shade. Reeds swayed around the water's circumference and the surrounding trees sat in silence, reflected off the surface of the pond. Emma sat down at the edge of a small dock worn with age, her legs dangling off the side, bare feet brushing the water. Taking a swig of Mountain Dew, she said, "Peaceful."

"Quite," William agreed. He stood next to her, looking across the fine stretch of water, toward the rustling reeds opposite them. They remained silent for a moment, struck by the beauty and solidarity of nature. Then Emma spoke up.

"Who's that?" she asked, pointing to one of the paths behind the pond, shaded by a collection of tall trees. A petite figure was walking in their direction, chemically-harmed hair swaying behind her in a high ponytail. Cassie walked toward them, a blinding white smile plastered to her smooth skin. Emma glared at William, who could only shrug sympathetically, as if to say he had no idea where she had come from.

"Hey, Will," Cassie said as she approached, shuffling across the dock to his side. "It's funny that you'd be here."

If voices had a taste, William thought, hers would taste like Splenda. Sweet, but fake.

"It's funny, because we live here," Emma muttered, receiving a warning glare from William.

"Hey, Cassie," William said, nervously, trying desperately to avoid eye contact. "What are you doing here?" The question sounded harmless, but inside he felt suddenly defensive. Why was she walking around in his neighborhood alone? She didn't live here, and thus, in his mind, didn't belong here.

Cassie grinned, the corners of her mouth twitching up. "Oh, come on," she said, with a playful smack to Williams arm. "I can be here if I want."

"No, you can't," Emma mumbled, even softer than before. "You don't live here." She turned her glaring eyes from William to the water.

Cassie scowled for a moment.

"Anyway, I was thinking we could hang out or talk or something," Cassie went on, glowing. "Unless you're otherwise preoccupied."

William scratched his head, trying hard not to focus on Emma's angry glower, which seemed to have the intention of boring steak knives into his face. "Right. Um, I'm pretty busy right now, actually."

"Standing on a dock?" Cassie raised her eyebrows.

"Spending time with my best friend," William said, defensively. He hadn't meant to sound mean, but he did unintentionally. "But I can spare a minute," he added quickly. Emma rolled her eyes.

"Whatever," she spat, standing up. "I've got to be home soon, anyway. Have fun, kids." William winced slightly, watching Emma walk off with a chug of her soda. He had just plunged into a deep ocean of awkward.

"Someone's a little salty," Cassie said, sounding annoyed, her eyes following Emma's carefree steps away from them.

"I'm not," William was looking at her skin. It was flawless, even under the makeup.

"I wasn't talking about you."

"Oh." William was now treading in the awkward ocean, trying to keep his head above water, but with no land in sight. "Well, she's just a little cranky sometimes. Don't take it personally."

Cassie pushed her bangs aside, one hand on her hip. "Are you two, like, a thing?"

This question didn't catch William particularly off-guard, considering how frequently it came up. He had heard it from his friends on many occasions, even from his teachers and his family. Complete strangers who happened to come across him and Emma hanging out had asked him before, yet with each inquiry it grew a little bit more irritating.

William shook his head. "Never. She's practically my sister."

"You're always together," Cassie continued.

"We're not a thing," William repeated, as he always did. "My best friend is a girl, that's all. It happens sometimes."

"Okay." There was a shade of uncertainty in her otherwise sweet voice, but Cassie's suspicions seemed mostly to have blown over. She sat herself on the edge of the dock prudishly, the bottoms of her shoes creating ripples on the water. Her yellow tank top was adorned with lace. It somehow seemed slightly more modest than her usual getup.

"I have a question," she stated quickly, as if she had to force the words out of her mouth. William felt a rush of heat pass over his body, and his mind began racing.

*"Please don't ask if I like you,"* he silently begged. *"I'd hate to say no."* Taking a moment to regain his lost composure, William shrugged. "What's up?" was all he said. Cassie turned to him, her long ponytail flipping over her shoulder.

"I talked to Kris this morning," she began, and William instantly felt a growing dread inside his stomach. If Kris was involved, he was automatically screwed over. "He said he was out last night, driving around, you know. Doing Kris stuff."

"*Illegal stuff,*" William mused silently, raising his eyebrows.

"He said he saw you," Cassie concluded.

William stiffened. "Oh." He racked his brain for a possible excuse, mortified that someone had seen him walking around at night. "Well, we were both at James'." He looked to Cassie for approval, but she didn't show any.

"I mean, he said he saw you later. Like, really early in the morning, just kind of walking around outside." Her eyes pierced him.

"I wasn't outside this morning," William lied. "That's weird. Why would I just be walking around?" He put on his best convincing face, which wasn't very convincing.

"Maybe it wasn't you, then."

"It wasn't me," he assured her. "That's just weird." It sounded funny to him, denying the existence of his most recurrent pastime, almost like a game. Overdo it, and she would become even more suspicious. Underdo it, and she would believe it was really him.

"Alright, I was just wondering," Cassie turned back to the water. "Because that would be pretty senseless, wandering around at night. Not very safe." William nodded in agreement, though replaying the previous night's event through his head. There had been that car, he remembered, speeding down the road. Perhaps he hadn't disappeared in time. If Kris had seen him, hell would be released from its moorings and set loose into his life.

"Yeah, definitely not me," William said. "I'm the epitome of safety, anyway."

"True," Cassie stifled a small laugh. She crossed her arms together, flicking a few drops of water across the pond with her shoe. They skipped across the surface and fell indefinitely into the infinity.

William, who had felt momentarily saved, felt a fresh rush of guilt flow through his body, and in one instant his thoughts flew from his mouth before he could pull them back.

"I feel bad," he began, and the rest of his words were flung from his mind violently. "I shouldn't have done what I did – what we did, last night. I know I probably seemed awfully convincing, but I kind of got caught in the moment and I just don't..." William paused, staring into Cassie's wide eyes. "...like you. I mean, of course I like you. I'm just not trying to start anything. You know?" William winced, looking pained as Cassie stared at him, expressionless. "It's just complicated."

"It's funny," Cassie said, standing up, "because I thought you weren't a dick."

William sighed. "Cass, come on."

"Don't call me that."

"Sorry." William cursed himself. "It really wasn't my intention to make you hate me, or to dick you like that."

"Well done," she huffed, crossing her arms. "You're supposed to be the nice one."

William sighed, shaking his head. "Well, it can't be entirely my fault, can it?" he said, with mild exasperation in his voice. "I didn't just make out with myself." William frowned at the expanse of his own stupidity.

"Oh, cool!" Cassie's grin was covered with scorn. "It looks like it's my fault. When does that ever happen?" she snapped, the sarcasm leaking liberally from her voice. "This is shaping up to be just another pity story. The insecure girl who likes the nice guy is let down upon knowing that he only hooked up with her for the thrill of it, with no intention of starting any sort of relationship."

William was taken aback, having to suppress a snort upon hearing "insecure," though with no intent to hastily apologize to Cassie. "Look," he said, moving a little closer. "Don't yell like that in public, it's weird."

Cassie rolled her eyes, angrily. "And don't try to make me the bad guy in this situation, because I'm not. You brought this upon yourself. If you want a real relationship in the future, don't start with something stupid like hooking up at a party. That'll get you nowhere."

"Come on, Will. Aren't you supposed to be decent?" Cassie exclaimed, and William's breath caught for a moment. "I've never seen you like this. You definitely aren't the guy I thought you were." She sighed, and walked away slowly.

Acting purely on impulse and a sudden rush of anger swimming in his blood, William called out to her, "You're right. Maybe if you had taken the time to get to know me instead of my mouth, you'd know who I really was." Cassie stopped suddenly and turned back to him, seeming suddenly more vulnerable and delicate. Her blue eyes were wide. "A quick tip for your next man," he added.

William certainly didn't expect Cassie to burst into an untimely flood of tears and most assuredly didn't know how to act in that situation. He could only think to stand completely still and look on while she spoke through choked sobs.

"You're right, damn it," she said, soft and full of real feelings. "I'm a slut, aren't I?"

William somehow managed to find the strength to stay silent.

"I haven't had a real relationship in years, because I just didn't care if a guy was using me or not. I'm notorious for hooking up." She wiped a couple of tears away, her hand blackened by damp makeup.

William sighed, his empathy returning to him. "Come on, Cassie. You're not like that," he said, as convincingly as he could, though it didn't appear to be much help.

"Shut up," Cassie sniffed. "Shut the hell up, Will, you're wrong. You're the same as everyone else. The guy is right and the girl is just another whore."

Though he felt a strong urge to comfort her, William couldn't find any consoling words for Cassie as she walked off, fuming.

He could have lied, and told her he did like her and sink into a whole new situation of trouble for her sake, but he couldn't bring himself to. For once he wanted to defend himself and he had. And he hated himself for it.

William walked home the opposite way from where he lived, taking the longer route for isolation purposes. It was a still afternoon; the sky was neutral, neither blue nor grey, the kind of color where it was impossible to tell where the clouds were or if they were there at all. He smelled clean-cut grass, though the air was silent, aside from the echo of his footsteps, beating lightly on the the sidewalk. He looked up only when he passed Leila's house, which looked lonely behind its sheet of foliage.

William knew that he hoarded a secret stigma, not of a bad quality but of a tendency to be too nice, and in the modern world that so easily manipulated him, kindness was weak and dying out. He would sacrifice his own manliness in regards to someone's feelings. He always apologized first. The chivalrous were a dying race and William, who was one of them, needed to escape to survive no matter how much his conscience disapproved.

He was making progress. Instead of giving in to Cassie to preserve her feelings, William had defended himself instead. He was making progress, and he wasn't proud.

He worried about Cassie, and he worried about Kris. Kris had seen him, he was sure of it, and now Kris would know that he had treated Cassie the way he had and undoubtedly, Kris would not approve. Kris, with his drugs and his name spelled with a K, wouldn't care that William had given up an opportunity to be nice. He would only care that William had hurt a girl who had put herself up to be hurt.

William passed his favorite tree on the walk home, and reached a delicate hand up to touch its branches, his fingers brushing the rough, therapeutic surface. It stood right beside the path, its branches arching elegantly over the sidewalk while its roots dug deep below. It was always bare, though that didn't make it any less beautiful. William couldn't describe exactly why it was his favorite tree, though he knew that if trees could speak, they would tell great stories. This tree would tell the best ones.

William thought about Emma, Cassie and Kris. He worried about them, and what they would think about him. He worried that Emma was slipping away, slowly. He worried about having enough time to get his homework done that night, then had to remind himself that it was Saturday. He worried that he was worrying too much.

He made his way home slowly and let himself in the sliding door to be greeted by two overwhelmingly loving dogs. He crept down the hallway and into his room, shutting the door silently. William lay down in bed with a book, and stayed there for a long time.

# EIGHT

William read until the day died, stopping only to pretend to sleep. He finished *The Two Towers* before seven and started on *The Return of the King* right as his mom burst into the room, disrupting his carefully balanced ambiance of peace and literature.

"William, are you coming out? It's dinner time," she said, walking over to the window, drawing the curtains back and opening it up halfway. William took his eyes off the page to gaze outside, where the sky was just beginning to darken. His next door neighbor was walking home with his dog and the voices of a friendly neighborhood wafted in, as did the smells of spring and summer. The noise of the highway a mile away echoed quietly.

"No, I'm not hungry," he told her, turning back to Gandalf and Pippin, who were riding across the countryside.

"You've been in here all day," she protested, hands on her hips. "Are you feeling okay?"

"Yup," William said. "I'm just not hungry, and a little tired." William's mom said okay, that there would be leftovers in the fridge in case he changed his mind, and left to greet William's father as he walked in the door. Well out of earshot of his parents, William let out an audible sigh. His mom hated when he sighed. Immersing himself back into the deep water of words, he read until midnight.

He should have been tired, but he was restless after spending the day cooped up inside his sanctuary, fidgety and unable to concentrate. He was anxious: worried about how Cassie felt, how Kris would react when he inevitably found out, why Emma had been acting so much more hostile than usual. His mind was jumbled, almost as cluttered as the empty, old cooking pot which sat under his bed, unused other than for the purpose of holding all of his poems. They were overflowing, neglected of proper organization as many were only scribbles of words on crumpled paper, no titles or dates. Memories of memories.

He got out of bed noiselessly, as he always did, setting the book down gently. He pulled the gray hoodie on. The night air blew gingerly through his window and it was quiet. Quiet, but not still. The night was always alive, always moving underneath the darkness. After you were out long enough, you would realize that it wasn't silent; there was sound, muffled by a dark, shadowy quilt. It was mobile and animate, softly swaying trees and fluttering leaves, life within the darker hours.

William stepped outside and shut the door with a soft *click*, immediately blanketed by the velvet nighttime quilt. When the world was asleep, he felt the world was his. When no one was there to see him, he was the person he always wanted to be. Reborn, night after night.

He wandered down a lonely bike path, touching his favorite tree on the way. He could finally think in peace and think fully, even worry to the best of his ability. It was safe at night.

Taking a short rout across a few unsuspecting neighbor's lawns, William made his way up to his school, which was sitting lonely and unattended, looming over a desolate, dark parking lot. He liked his school when no one was in it. William jogged lightly across a wide grass field, coming up to the deserted brick walls which stood cold and unmoving, characteristics generally associated with brick walls. They seemed much less menacing at night, like they had some regard for William's feelings, apologizing for confining him during the week.

"It's okay," he whispered to the walls. "It's not you."

William moved on, walking the perimeter of the building before returning to the parking lot. He lay on his back, hands folded across his stomach while his eyes gazed upwards, only able to count one star. He breathed easily and blinked slowly, the night air enveloping him in a comforting embrace, one that could only be found at this time, in an unlikely place. William's eyes searched the domed sky, looking for something unknown, whether it be a shooting star, or a plane in the distance. Maybe he was searching for God. He was enveloped in his own serenity, completely peaceful and solitary.

"Fancy seeing you here," a voice like summer nipped at William's neck and he lurched back suddenly, attempting to jump up but only managing to scoot back a few inches.

"Holy shit."

Leila chuckled, standing a few feet away with her arms crossed. "Sorry. I can't lie; I actually was trying to scare you. It was the perfect opportunity."

"Holy shit," William said again, standing up. His atmosphere had shattered, suddenly. "Jeez, I thought you were here to kill me."

"No. But that might happen if you continue napping in the middle of parking lots." The corners of Leila's mouth twitched skyward.

William was completely taken aback, focusing too hard on Leila to speak. He always imagined her to be delicate to the extent that she would shatter at any point of human contact, but as he saw her now, she didn't seem that way. Here, at midnight, she had a new aura of confidence, as if she owned the night time. She stood in her bare feet and sweatpants, but most prominently a plain white T-shirt. It may have been the first time William had ever seen her in short sleeves. She looked strong, athletic.

"I didn't expect too many cars in the school parking lot around this time," William admitted, his blue eyes catching a glimpse of Leila's dark brown ones.

"Kind of like how you don't expect to see too many people in the school parking lot around this time?" she suggested, raising an eyebrow inquisitively. William felt his face flush.

"Well, yeah. Exactly. Honestly, on a scale of one to coincidence, this is like a twelve."

Leila laughed, a sound like crackling leave. "I know. I figured one encounter was pretty weird, but I guess there aren't too many people enjoy midnight meanders."

"Midnight meanders," William said, staring at the sky. "That could be a kick-ass band name." He chuckled to himself.

"Indie rock?" Leila mused.

"Most definitely."

Leila sat down, brushing the hair out of her eyes, and asked, "How often are you out here?" Her dark eyes pierced William.

"A few times a week," he admitted, sitting across from her. "What about you?"

"Almost every night." She had no shame. "Insomnia."

"Oh," William didn't know what to say. "I hit trees."

"What?" Leila was confounded

"Well, I'm not trying to hurt them," William admitted, embarrassed. "I don't do it anymore. It was just sort of a de-stressor."

"A really fruitless one," Leila added.

"Yeah. All that happened was I bled a lot. Midnight meanders are a lot more substantial. They make me feel better than butchering my hand." Leila was snickering.

"I'm sorry. Can we be like, an exclusive club? The Midnight Meander-ers?" she mused, shaking her head. A few strands of red hair fell out of her ponytail. Her voice was like summer, and her hair like autumn.

"People might mistake us for tree-hitting insomniacs, William protested, drawing a warm smile out of Leila.

"Good one."

They sat in silence for a moment, with Leila looking at the stars and William staring at the ground. Questions pounded at the gate of his mind, each one knocking at the edges of his temples, setting his mind into a frenzy. He had never seen Leila speak so much, or with so much self-assurance. At school she was almost always silent, yet now she was talking to him and telling him about herself and having no shame whatsoever. She was wearing short sleeves. He itched to ask her.

"How come you never talk in school?" he started, her eyes flickering over to him. "I mean, I never really hear you. I didn't know you would be so inclined to carry on a conversation in such...different circumstances."

"What, sitting outside in the middle of the night?" she asked, blasé.

"Yeah."

Leila shifted uncomfortably and puffed out her cheeks, exhaling. "I don't know," she admitted. "I just feel a little more at ease out here, oddly enough. It's a whole other world at night, and I like it. There's no one there to judge you."

"Judge you for what?" William inquired.

"Anything."

William let this soak in. He felt the same way, though he wasn't sure if he was going to admit it or not. It was another world, where living things pulsed and inhaled the rhythmic flow of breathing air. Trees would listen, and the road he walked on would listen to his quiet footsteps, as would the birds that lay awake and the humming, invisible insects. They didn't judge, and they didn't ask questions. They only listened.

"Huh," he suddenly felt an irrevocable respect towards her. She, who he finally understood was so like himself, would understand the poems and the tree-hitting and the empty feelings. The longing for something he didn't know existed quite yet. "I hear that."

It was Leila's turn to inquire. "No headphones tonight?" she asked the ground.

"Oh." William had completely forgotten. "Today was just kind of a weird day. I didn't really stick to routine, you know?"

Leila gazed at him, slim features searching his. "Something wrong?" she asked.

"Nah."

"You sure?"

"Nah," William admitted with a passive sigh. "But it'll be alright. Shit happens. It's not a big thing." He tried to shrug off Leila's inquisitive glances. Her eyes were mesmerizing.

"You can tell me," she pursued. "We're the midnight meander-ers, after all. What happens in the parking lot at this hour isn't really bound to go anywhere."

"I hooked up with a girl I didn't like," he admitted. To say this to anyone else might have seemed foolish to William, but he knew from Leila's voice that she wasn't one to judge or tell secrets. "So I kind of dicked her and now I feel pretty bad, but I had to stand up for myself. It's something I never do. It felt good, now that I think of it, but I'm just afraid of the consequences."

Leila nodded, slowly and thoughtfully, giving William a look that made his stomach mix. "Well, congratulations then. Defending one's honor is a tough task for some, myself included. It feels hella nice, though, doesn't it?"

William let go a natural smile. "Definitely."

"Don't worry about the outcome. People might give you crap, but you know you were right, right?"

"Sure."

"Good man." She nodded.

There was a pause in the conversation, and William wanted so badly to hear her voice. He was afraid if he stopped talking, she would disappear as silently as she came.

"Um," he started, but closed his mouth, suddenly self-conscious. Leila reached up to brush a lock of hair out of her eyes and as she did so William caught sight of her inner forearm, bare and bleeding. He blinked. Leila seemed not to have noticed. "You're bleeding," he said blankly, straining his eyes.

"What?" Leila said, as if oblivious.

William nodded at her. "Your arm's bleeding, I think. You alright?"

Leila looked quizzical and confused for a moment, then suddenly concerned. A thin glaze covered her eyes for a moment.

William saw her stricken for an instant, saw her breath catch, but she shrugged it off and folded her arms. "Oh. It's all good."

William raised an eyebrow with growing concern. "Are you sure?" he asked, staring into Leila's face, the composure of which was suddenly broken. "How'd that happen?"

Leila stared needles back at him. "We just got a new cat," she said. "He's cute and everything, but he's a monster."

She was lying, William could tell. "Did someone try to hurt you?"

"Yeah," Leila rolled her eyes. "My cat. His name is Evgeni and he always tries to fight me. I'm forced to take him down against my own pacifist beliefs." Sarcasm leaked from her stare.

William was distracted from his concern for a moment. "You named your cat Evgeni?" he asked, skeptical.

"Russian pride," she answered.

"Malkin or Nabokov?" William asked, with a wry smile.

"Plushenko."

William sniggered. "Are you even Russian?" he asked. He realized he was straying from the situation at hand to Leila's obvious relief, but decided to drop it. If it was nothing, it was nothing.

"A quarter," Leila said, loosening up a little. She held her shoulders high again. Her posture was excellent. "You can't really tell. I don't speak Russian or anything."

William shrugged. "No big. I don't speak Hebrew. You'd only know I was Jewish by the amount of bagels I consume in a day."

"I guess I've never seen you eat bagels, then." Leila smiled. "I didn't know you were Jewish."

William nodded, rolling his eyes with a wry smile. "No one does."

"Well, same goes with me. I'm just that gorgeous, super talented ginger girl without a soul."

"The one who only talks at midnight in the school parking lot."

"Precisely." Leila looked up at the moon, a pearly voice against velvet sky. "Parking lots are nice and all, but do you wanna walk?"

# NINE

"Have you ever thought about being caught?" Leila asked, padding lightly across the sidewalk. "Like, what would you do if someone found you right now? I mean, besides me." She had her arms folded across her T-shirt, hair entangled in the breeze. Her brown eyes stared straight ahead, though not harshly.

William contemplated this, although he had thought it over many times before.

"I'd probably fight them," he said in very little seriousness, looking at Leila out of the corner of his eye. "Just, you know, so they know not to screw with me in the future." He saw Leila roll her eyes with a grin.

"Good plan."

William snorted. "Thanks." He walked on the right of Leila, his head held up unlike hers. "No, that's not true. I guess I'd probably tell them not to worry about it, if it was a friend. If it was a stranger I think I'd just take the chance and run. If it were a cop, I'd probably make up some ridiculous story about getting lost or needing to blow off steam. I'd only fight them if desperate measures needed to be taken." He ran a hand through his own auburn hair. "I guess it would be a rather impromptu decision."

Leila nodded, wearing her own vague expression of recognition. "What if it was your mom?"

William shrugged, scuffing the backs of his shoes on the ground.

"I'm sure I could successfully make up a bullcrap excuse. After all, I have years of experience in that field." His mouth twitched up into goofy smile. "Sorry, Mom. School really stresses me out, this is the only way to keep myself from worrying." Although they sounded right in his head, the words that came out of his mouth were actually a prime example of why he *did* walk. Before he could change his wording, Leila spoke instead.

"That sounds a lot like you, William, I'm sure she'd buy it," she told him, with a palpably humorous wink.

"Yeah? And what's your good excuse?" William challenged, crossing his arms as they simultaneously made a ceremonial walking stop at a stop sign.

"I've got plenty," she retaliated as they began walking again. "They include, but are not limited to, I'm sorry officer, but I was at this sleepover and they asked me if I wanted a drink and I didn't feel comfortable. The only way home was walking and I didn't want to wake up my parents." She looked at William for feedback. He only shook his head.

"Weak."

"What?" Leila scoffed.

"It's a weak excuse!" William grinned, shaking his head. Leila made a face at him.

"It's better than running!" she reciprocated, lowering her voice quickly after. "Well, maybe we shouldn't yell. But still! Cops dig the whole not-drinking shit. Maybe I'd even get a ride home in a cop car, sirens going off and all."

William laughed. "Now you're just getting your hopes up." He smiled at Leila's derisive face with amusement.

"No, you're wrong," she went on, despite his snippy comments. "Cops are more likely to believe a kid who's not giving into peer pressure, as opposed to one who's running from them. Come at me, bro." She held her arms out in a come-at-me-bro manner. William gave a half-hearted snort.

"On a scale of one to crappy, that idea is a twelve," he replied, shrugging. "But, whatever you say. If you aren't capable of outrunning the police, leave it to me."

Leila opened her mouth, her eyes full of delight. "Is that a challenge?" she asked, with a grin. "I'm not a bad runner, you know."

William smiled crookedly, sauntering with his hands on his hips. "Neither am I," he suggested. "I've got to be pretty in shape for soccer." There was an unceremonious and unnecessary flexing of the biceps, an action that caused a rolling of eyes out of Leila.

"And when was the last time you played soccer with your arms?" she coaxed.

"You know what I mean."

"I'll bet I could bench more than you anyway." Leila's smile grew and she laughed out loud upon seeing William's bemused expression. "No, I'm just messing with you. I always lacked in the upper body strength department."

William looked at her. "Probably because you're so damn skinny." She laughed with obvious sarcasm.

"Let's not go there," she said, decorated by a smug grin.

William didn't quite understand, as she didn't have even an ounce of fat on her body. He simply shook his head.

"Why do girls always think they're fat?" he inquired. She gave him an indescribable look: a combination of self-sympathy and secrecy.

"Girls don't think they're fat," she said, gazing toward the sky. "They just think they're not skinny enough. Just like they don't think they're pretty enough or funny or talented enough. They don't think they're enough of anything. I guess that's one of the many disadvantages of being a teenager. You aren't enough of anything to be a whole person."

William blinked his green eyes a few times. "That was deep," he admitted.

"Not really. That's just life," Leila said with a shrug. She turned suddenly, and bolted down an adjacent street, running in the shadows below the streetlamps.

William was stunned for a moment, before he smiled and sprinted after her, his legs flying easily. She breezed in front of him, bright hair trailing behind her like a wispy string of smoke that William could not catch, no matter how fast he pushed himself. They splashed through puddles with reckless intent until Leila reached the end of the street and stopped, resting beside a large oak tree while William lumbered in behind her, flopping himself down onto the ground.

"Didn't I say I could run, Mr. Soccer Prodigy?" she said.

William buried his face in his hands, breathing hard. "Good lord. I didn't realize you were a regular antelope," he panted, pushing a few strands of hair out of his eyes. Leila was standing over him, her right hand offered out. He let her help him up.

"Well, when there's a giant, inescapable void where your social life should be, there isn't much else to do but run, sleep and read." Leila smirked, tying her hair back into a loose ponytail. William was just beginning to notice that she smelled faintly like the springtime; flowers and trees and fresh grass intertwined with the smell of charcoal pencils and art. He realized he was holding his breath.

"I would give up a lot if I could just read all day," William admitted, shrugging his shoulders deeper into his grey hoodie. "Sometimes I do that during the summer, when I can just sit outside for hours. It's like getting lost, but in words." He silently cursed himself for sounding so stupid, though Leila seemed to have taken no notice of his lack of eloquence.

"It's heavenly," she said, her red hair and her springtime-artsy scent making up all the magnificent cells of her person. "Writing, too. It's pretty inspiring to write outside."

William looked at her with narrow eyes. "You write?"

"I write things," she answered. "I figure everyone writes words, though not everyone writes things extensive enough to be considered writing."

With a rush of uncontrollable reaction, William blurted out, "I write poems." He felt like the world paused for just a moment. The birds and the insects and the ongoing traffic noise from a nearby highway held their breath for a second. This second, William took note of as he looked nervously to Leila for a reaction, took far longer than a normal second would. It stared him in the face and mocked him.

"Really?" she questioned. William nodded, silent. The birds and insects and traffic noise commenced again suddenly as he breathed. "Oh. I didn't think I'd ever meet a guy who'd admit that." She smiled, gazing at the ground. "That's really cool, actually. I respect that a lot."

"Yeah, well." William scratched his head out of nervous habit. "It's just a hobby and all that. Nothing big."

"Why do you do it?"

"For the same reason I walk."

There was clear evidence of understanding in Leila's face as she nodded and looked at the ground. William felt extremely conscious suddenly, not only of himself but also of his surroundings and, more importantly, the time of day; or, rather, night. Pulling his phone out of his pocket, William checked the time.

"Dude," he said. "It's like, one-thirty." Leila frowned.

"Shit, for real?" she asked, one eyebrow raised. "I think I was trying to get back home by one."

"Oh," William looked apologetically over at her. "My fault." She only shook her head, hastening her step slightly.

"It's all good. I think I should probably just head home now, though. You should too, we got school Monday. You might as well get a little sleep. You need to be properly rested to be properly edumacated," she said with a smile and a raise of her delicate eyebrows.

William was expressionless. "Well," she continued, "This has been interesting and a little bit weird, but I'm glad it happened. I'll see you tomorrow, Will."

As Leila gave a final smile and turned to walk back, William called, "Hey, Leila?" She turned, looking at him, expectantly. He felt suddenly nervous. "Are you sure you're okay?"

Leila frowned. "What do you mean?"

"You were bleeding, I think," he said, burying his hands in his pockets almost in an attempt to bury himself in them as well. Leila shook her head.

"I wasn't. I'm fine," she told him. "I'm great. See you."

William watched her walk away for a minute, half out of curiosity and half protectiveness, until she turned down a narrow street and disappeared from his sight. The air was a little chillier than it had been and both his body and his mind felt mildly shitty, unable to adjust to the changing temperatures. He felt enlightened in a way, yet still completely clueless about Leila. The more she exposed her personality, the less he found he knew about her.

He took the bike path home, which he usually never did. The main roads were more comforting at night, with the street lamps standing guard and all of the sleeping houses there to guide your way. The bike path through the woods, however, provided William with an invigorating sense of reality after his unusual encounter, though he was sure that a wild bear or a serial killer was bound to jump out and kill him at some point. This notion did not possess his mind quite as much as the ginger girl who he had just spent the night with, in the nonsexual and literal sense.

She was right handed and her left arm had been bleeding.

William recalled a memory from the back of his consciousness and slipped it into the movie reel of his mind, being swept away into the past as it played back to him. It was Halloween in seventh grade, and his friend Ryan had decided to test the epitome of douchebaggery, doing so by dressing in black and slathering fake blood all over his wrists.

"Look, dude," he told William, displaying an irksome smile of pleasure. "I'm so emo. Life is so hard." With that he took a butter knife and pretended to slash away at his arms, making William's stomach churn.

Recalling this, William resisted the urge to plunge his fist into the nearest tree, imagining that it resembled Ryan's ungrateful face that would soon be coated with his own blood. His resistance took all of the mental stamina he possessed.

Coming up to his backyard, William strayed from the bike path and onto his porch, sliding the door open without a sound. Damian picked his head up from the couch to acknowledge William, who was already making his way to his room with every intent of collapsing onto his bed. William fell asleep instantly.

# TEN

"Dude, you're a dick." William was only half awake when Kris' frank insult permeated his eardrums. He turned slowly to look into the enormous junior's face, which might have seemed menacing if his constant clueless expression wasn't in the way. "Pardon?" William asked, shuffling through the crowded hallways on his first period English class that Monday morning, Kris glued to his side.

"Come on, Spencer. You know what you did."

William laughed out loud momentarily at being addressed by his last name. It was intended to sound more patronizing than it actually did. "No, not really. Enlighten me, perhaps?" It could have been his obvious exhaustion, with the added obscurity of the previous night's events, but for whatever reason, William was being uncharacteristically bold, especially toward his older, larger in stature and slightly more intimidating teammate. Kris only glared.

"Cassie told me everything you said to her, kid," he said coldly. "Hey, Josh," he nodded to a friend of his as they passed in the hallway, but turned his icy stare back to William. "You totally led her on. That's not okay."

William, almost amused, raised an eyebrow at Kris. "So you, of all people, are going to get mad at me for hooking up with a girl when I had no intention of dating her?" The purple skin under his eyes made William look even more sarcastic.

"Cassie's my friend," Kris growled. "I'm not gonna have you doing that to my friends."

William snorted. "Okay, so a guy can hook up with a girl he doesn't really care about, but the minute he hooks up with your friends you have a problem? Is that what you're implying?" William answered his own question for Kris. "Yes, it is, showing that you are hypocritical and wrong and have no reason at all to be mad at me. Yeah, I dicked her, and I feel bad about it. But that isn't your problem, nor is it your concern." Catching the blank expression on Kris' face, he motioned for the monster to leave. "You can go."

Kris' eyes bore into him, a solid twelve on the scale from one to furious, and William could imagine him taking a hammer to his skull without any second thought.

"Don't try me with your big words," he said before marching off.

William watched him skulk down the hallway, shoving an unsuspecting freshman to the side.

The bell rang and ushered William into class, where he went immediately to his desk and sat attentively, as opposed walking over to a tightly knit group of his friends who were huddled in a corner, like he normally would have. Sitting by himself, he waited the abnormally long five minutes until the late bell rang and around him, his peers started to fill into their seats.

"Hey, Will," Anthony, a casual acquaintance of William's said, sitting down beside him. Anthony was hardcore about lacrosse as well as wearing plaid on Thursdays.

"Hey, man." William nodded as his English teacher, Mr. Monroe, started handing back essays from the previous week: reflections on the symbolism from George Orwell's 1984. William had written about the rats. "You have a good weekend?"

Anthony nodded as a paper landed on his desk. Anthony, as far as William could tell from Mr. Monroe's sarcastic comments, had written about the victory coffee and had managed to go off on a reckless tangent about how companies like Starbucks were monopolizing small businesses and putting many people out of jobs. William remembered that Anthony's mom owned a little coffee shop.

"It was pretty cool. I feel pretty cruddy though; I didn't get to sleep until late. I guess that's what you get for not starting your homework until Sunday night." Anthony laughed.

William nodded in agreement, trying not to appear too disgruntled. Too many people complained about staying up late. "Yeah, I hear that." William's essay fluttered down onto his desk as Mr. Monroe shuffled away to distribute more papers. Picking it up, Willism William read,

*"Good analysis of the rats as ghosts of Winston's past. Excellent word choice and overall grammatical understanding."*

"Huh. I got an A," he said, satisfied. From what he remembered, he bullshitted the entire essay, making sure to include a quote from *Fight Club*, as he did with every English essay he had written that year.

"I didn't," Anthony said, with a snort. "I guess that's the result of feeling passionately about coffee."

William smiled, and focused his attention on Mr. Monroe for as long as he could before his mind drifted off. The total came to about forty-seven seconds. They had already poured over *1984* for weeks, tearing apart each sentence and each word with the intent of finding the meaning behind every letter that Orwell wrote. William felt that George Orwell would not be very pleased to learn that his book wasn't being read as much as it was being dismantled. If William himself ever wrote a novel, he wouldn't want people analyzing it so precisely.

"Oh, by the way," Anthony's voice whispered over the drone of a class discussion. "Did you really hook up with Cassie?"

Upon hearing these words, William was tempted to slam his head down onto the desk face first with the strength of a wildebeest. Instead, he did so with the strength of only a small cow, a muffled *thunk* resonating through the classroom. He could feel every head in the room turning to look at him, perplexed, before they shook it off and went back to either learning, texting, or sleeping.

"Yes, I did. I don't want to talk about it."

"Holy shit, dude," Anthony said, almost appalled.

"Are they still looking at me?" William's muffled voice said.

Mr. Monroe's voice came in response.

"Will?"

"Yep?"

Mr. Monroe scratched his head while a few more students looked on. "Are you okay?" he asked, obvious perplexity in his voice.

"Yes." William did not pick his head up for a few seconds, until he was sure that everyone in the room had lost interest in him.

"There's a huge red mark on your face," were Anthony's words.

"Yes, I hooked up with Cassie. I kind of dicked her because I don't like her. Let's not talk about it, please."

Anthony looked ever so confused. "Well, congrats," he said, with a chuckle. "That's not really such a bad thing."

"Yes, it is."

Anthony shrugged and turned his focus to the front of the room.

William slumped back in his chair and looked as if he were paying attention for the next forty-seven minutes. At this current moment in time, he did not care for the English language. He didn't care for participial phrases or George Orwell's prediction of communist governments. He didn't care about caring. The only thing he could care to care about seemed to be Leila.

After first period, William was the first one out of Mr. Monroe's door and the first one to enter his second period computer science class. In the minute that it took him to make the trek, three more people asked him about Cassie. Likewise, on his way to Chemistry after second period, four more brought the subject up. A few people, including Cassie, yelled at him about Cassie.

William skipped lunch after third period, hiding out in the library instead so as to avoid any more confrontation that he didn't desire to face and by the time he got to his fourth period class he was beat, not only from his obvious lack of sleep and energy, but from having to dart around the hallways to evade his curious friends.

Hawthorne River High School ran an A-Day, B-Day schedule, meaning that students alternated fourth period classes every day. The problem with fourth period was that fourth period sucked. Lasting for an hour and a half, all hope of maintaining any meager amount of focus was lost after the first thirty minutes. When William ducked into Journalism hoping to go unnoticed, he was caught, as he was everyday, by Emma.

"Hey, dude," she said, greeting him as he walked in and accompanying him to his desk. "What's up? You look tired. How was your day?" William looked at her, exhausted.

"Good," he said, slumping into his chair. He put his head down, massaging his temples lightly.

"Oh, me too, thanks for asking." Emma said, rolling her eyes in all seriousness.

"Sorry," William grumbled. "I don't feel that good."

Emma grunted. "Do you ever?" she muttered.

William picked his head up, suddenly defensive. Adrenaline was a funny thing, he thought.

"What?" He narrowed his eyes, more out of confusion than anger.

Emma looked at him plainly, as if the answer should have been a little more obvious. "You never feel good. All you do is sleep and mope. Whenever I ask you to hang out, it's always, 'No, I'm taking a nap. No, I'm sad. No, I'm too tired.' Wake up!" she said, folding her arms.

William stared. "You're seriously mad at me?" he asked, raising his eyebrows. A few more students had walked in and were gathering around the scene. Emma clearly didn't mind the attention. She soaked it in and wallowed in it.

"Don't you think I have the right to get mad?" she asked. "It's like you never want to be around me anymore." As William opened his mouth in protest, she continued, "You know what, not even that. You seem like you don't want to be around anyone anymore. You dicked Cassie at the party, and then you dicked me for Cassie the next day. You're just so passive about everything. You're the passive bad guy. Does that even exist?"

William, taken aback felt his heart rate accelerate. His blood pounded at his veins and threatened to jump out of his skin. He physically could not control his mouth from opening and speaking.

"Well, apparently it does now, if that's what you're planning on saying about your best friend. Should I even say best friend? Do *those* even exist anymore?" A chorus of *oohs* swept around the classroom, though Emma only rolled her sharp blue eyes. "All you ever want to do is prove that you're right. Prove that you're more right than everyone else, especially me. I'm a little sick of it."

Emma's arms were folded tightly and her face was scrunched in frustration. "I'm a little sick of you." She was interrupted before she could finish.

"Ooh! Hold up, let me treat that burn," William said with all the frustration that had built up inside of him. "Clearly you are, because you don't even bother asking if I'm okay when I'm down, or asking why I'm so tired when I am. You don't even know me anymore," he finished. Emma forced a smile and nodded. "Did I ever?" she questioned. William only shrugged. "Fuck you, then." Emma stormed off to her seat as Mr. Schwartz, who slightly resembled Santa Claus, walked in with an assortment of paper falling out of his arms.

"Well, I could cut the tension in here with a chainsaw!" he said, painfully chipper. "Because it seems as if a butter knife would be insubstantial in this situation. Everything okay in here?"

"Fine," William and Emma answered. They avoided each other's glares.

Santa Claus smiled. "I can tell today's class is going to be excellent," he said.

# ELEVEN

For the first time that day, William did not rush to his next class at the ringing of the bell. He packed up slowly, purposefully as everyone filed out, shooting Emma one last angry glance. She returned the favor quickly.

"Bye, Mr. Schwartz," William said as he walked toward the door. Santa Claus beamed, shuffling through a stack of papers on his desk.

"Goodbye, William. Is everything okay with you and Emma?" he asked, scratching his beard. William forced a smile. "It's fine. Thanks," he tried, exiting the class before more questions could be asked. His mind was numb and with two more classes in the day, William wasn't sure he could make it. It seemed that Emma, Kris, Cassie, everyone who knew them currently wanted him to endure a punishment that was somewhat less harsh than death but still callous enough that he would be significantly unhappy for a long period of time. He didn't understand, particularly with Emma, how she had turned on him so quickly.

William walked into the art room, relieved to finally be in a tolerable place for the next hour. Though the late bell to fifth period hadn't yet rung, William was already dreading sixth.

Mrs Davis was at her desk, not giving a damn as usual and the sixteen other students that made up Art II were milling around purposelessly. James was napping in his seat and Leila was huddled in the back, nestled into a grey 'cross country' hoodie, both legs resting on the stool next to her. William walked over.

Leila looked up from the spot on the table she had been staring at to smile at William, dropping her legs from the stool and gesturing him over. Her red hair was tied up; a loose ponytail with a few strands hanging down that framed her face nicely.

"Hey," she said, smiling. "Would it be too cliché for me to say,

78

'long time, no see?'" Leila asked. William dropped himself onto the stool next to her and laid his head down on the table.

"It would make perfect sense," he muttered though the wood, face down. "As much sense as four times three being twelve. I'm the four, you're the three, twelve in the morning is when we didn't go to sleep. Get it?" William looked up long enough to see Leila staring at him, confused, until he put his head back down again.

"Well, someone's starting to speak a little gibberish," she said. "How tired are you?" William sighed and, sitting up straight again, looking into Leila's face.

"On a scale of one to about to hibernate, I'm a twelve." Leila looked away to hide her wry smile, to William's dismay. It was a pretty smile.

"Midnight meanderers don't need sleep!" she scolded. Across the room, Mrs. Davis was talking about something that didn't matter, and Leila went right on ignoring her. "Although, I've been hearing some nasty things about you throughout the day." William sighed, and planted his face right back on the paint-stained surface of the table. "Stuff about the Cassie situation. With all these things people are saying, I think you're deserving of a nap."

"Rumors circulate too fast here. It's like someone hears one thing and can instantly send it out to everyone else," William said.

Leila nodded in approval. "They're called Smartphones." She patted him on the back, making his skin jump. He was worried she could feel it, but her expression didn't change.

"Mr. Spencer, no sleeping in my class!" Mrs. Davis barked from the front of the room, completely ignoring James, who was still snoring at his seat.

"Sorry," William muttered, sitting up straight. He and Leila were silent for the next few minutes, while Mrs. Davis explained what their schedule for the day would look like; continue working on abstract self-portraits until they lost motivation or interest, and then sit and talk until the bell rang. William hadn't even started his portrait, he realized, as Leila got up to pull her own out from the drying rack.

He stared. It wasn't finished, but it looked as good, if not better, than any completed project. There was a rough charcoal outline of her face, with the neck and shoulders fading out gradually into the background: a velvet blue night sky hovering over a quiet street. Her right eye was a street lamp, lit dimly next to her closed left eye, a crescent moon. Trees growing around the edges of the paper intertwined with her hair, making soft autumn leaves grow out of each thin branch. A faint, jagged red line ran diagonally across the page.

"Good lord, woman," William said, shaking his head. "Stop being so talented," he teased, pulling a smile out of Leila.

"Well, maybe if you actually started yours…" she replied.

"Hey, I don't need your sass. This is what I really am," William said, in very little seriousness. "A white blank page." Leila nodded.

"Like that Mumford and Sons song?" she asked.

William smiled. "I didn't even think of that."

Leila got up to fetch a few brushes and some paint, milling about the room to talk to Mrs. Davis while William stared down at the empty, white page. It stared him back, uninspiring, and dull, apathetic and typical. *"Like me,"* he thought. *"Empty."* William always felt like he had an idea for his self-portrait somewhere in the back of his mind, but he could never single it out for himself. It was stuck there, waiting ever patiently for someone to pull it out while William fumbled for it around the edges, unsuccessful.

Leila was still up, finding her essential materials, so William, in a fit of frenzied emotions, walked over to sit with James, who was just waking up from his nap. James and William had been close acquaintances since middle school, and his decency and impartial attitude were enough for William to go to him, occasionally, for advice. James was like Hawthorne River's own Switzerland; he wouldn't take a side.

"Hey," William said, sliding into a seat next to James, the masculine smell of Axe suddenly overwhelming him. James' self portrait so far was astonishing; William couldn't tell exactly what was on the page, but it looked sort of like a faceless man playing a shiny pair of cymbals. The cymbals had pupils and irises, and William felt suddenly uncomfortable. James' portrait had a greater meaning than William cared to know about.

"Hello, Sir William," James said, in his drowsy, post-nap state. "How is this fine spring day treating you?" He looked to William with his usual blank expression.

"Fine. Shitty, actually," William admitted, glancing around the room. Leila was back at the table, wetting a few brushes. She had the same look of contentment on her face that she did the previous night, out in the parking lot at midnight. Art made her glow. "I don't know if you heard, but I'm Hawthorne's new bad guy, according to Cassie O'Brien." James pursed his lips and nodded, understandingly.

"Ah, yeah. I've been hearing some nasty things about you," he admitted to William's obvious resentment. "I don't really believe much of it. I know you hooked up with Cassie, but I didn't think the mono part was true..." William sighed loudly, throwing his face forcefully into his hands.

"Who the heck makes these things up?" he inquired, quite perturbed. "Mono, seriously? I give them one spot of dirt on my hands and they blow it up. Next thing you know, they'll tell you I was deported to Germany and died of the hiccups," William said, angrily. He felt a wave of frustration wash over him, causing him to shudder violently for a moment. In that moment, he had really wanted to hit something, preferably with his fist.

"Heard it through the grapevine," James admitted, truthfully. "I knew it wasn't right though. You're not a douchebag, William

Spencer." He smiled, and patted William on the back.

"Thanks, James," William said. "Uh, you aren't either."

"News spreads here almost as fast as swine flu paranoia did in 2009. It'll die down soon, okay?" James said, his voice reassuring. "If you need me to beat anyone up, say the word."

William nodded, smiling as he stood up again. "Thanks, James," he said again. "You rock. See you around."

"Peace." James fell promptly back asleep, smudging his cymbals.

William walked to the table in the back where Leila was sitting by herself, bobbing her head softly to the music coming from her headphones. As William sat down beside her, he popped one out of her ear and placed it in his own, being welcomed by a peaceful folk melody and a sarcastic rolling of the eyes from Leila.

"Oh, please, go ahead," she said, in a voice full of irony. "Feel no need to ask my permission."

William grinned, the corners of his mouth perking upward. "You're busy enough," he said, motioning toward her portrait. She was working on darkening the sky with a velvety violet. "I need the inspiration."

"Well, you could start by drawing yourself," Leila mused. "See where it goes from there." She looked to William and gave him a smile before directing her attention back to her own portrait.

The art room grew quiet after a few minutes; William could only hear the scratching of charcoal on paper and brushes being swirled around in water, along with the calming music coming out of Leila's headphones, one of which still stretched over to his own ear. Within a few minutes, William felt himself reflexively picking up a pencil and putting it to his own paper, sketching out the face that stared back at him from the small, sequined mirror on the table.

Wavy auburn feathers covered his head and the edges of the rough canvas of his face. His eyebrows looked disturbingly feminine as he scrawled them out, though they looked disappointingly similar to those in the mirror, arching softly over his deep-set eyes and dark lashes. The irises of his eyes weren't any color but green, though the bags beneath them were like translucent storm clouds. On his paper, William drew those same clouds below his eyes, raining onto the pale oceans of his cheeks.

William couldn't draw like Leila could, and his depth perception was a little bit wonky. When he painted, the colors muddled together to form undesirable shades. He didn't like oil pastels because they would smudge the decent charcoal skeleton that he had already created and watercolors bled. Aesthetically, William's artwork was average. Metaphorically, it was something else.

Words were his preferred media and poems were the outcome. You could see paintings and hear music and witness overdramatized soap operas, but you could feel words, and read them and believed them until they became what was really true. You could see them the way you would see a drawing, but with your mind instead of your eyes.

A small, dark figure peered out from each of the irises that William had drawn on his paper, blending into green, camouflaged eyes. The figure on the left looked inquisitive, peeking his head out in curiosity, while the one on the right hid himself behind a curtain of light that glanced off William's right eye.

"There are people in my eyes," William whispered, involuntarily. Leila raised a thin eyebrow.

"That didn't make any sense, did it?"

"Not at all," she replied, leaning over to investigate William's drawing so far. William felt the sudden urge to yank it away and tell her not to look, though he suppressed it.

"Oh, wow," Leila said. "There are people in your eyes." William felt self-conscious suddenly. He had put a considerable amount of effort into that drawing, and it still looked less than mediocre.

"It's not that good," he mumbled, mentally urging Leila to look away from it, though she just shook her head.

"It's better than you think it is, if you don't think it's that good," she said, though William could not help but think that she was mocking it in her mind.

"It's alright, I guess." William scratched his head, looking around the classroom so he wouldn't have to meet Leila's gaze. "It just doesn't really make any sense."

Leila shrugged, her dark brown eyes locked onto the portrait again.

"I'm sure it does, to you," she said, tilting her head slightly. "Unless you're suggesting that you didn't know what you were thinking, in which case I don't have a solution for you." She chuckled a bit to herself, though William still felt just as uncomfortable. He *hadn't* really known what he was thinking, he had just been drawing.

William's creative flow left him, and he didn't touch the drawing for the rest of class, except to put it away when the bell rang.

"Thanks for the music," he said, handing the headphone back to Leila, who smiled in acknowledgement.

"No problem." She picked her painting up delicately, turning her back on William as she walked toward the drying rack. William picked this moment to leave the classroom, looking back as he exited to see if Leila had turned around. She hadn't. He walked down the hallway to Spanish class, dreading the next hour, though he actually found it to be rather peaceful. He walked into the classroom and sat down in the back, and he didn't speak to anyone until the final bell rang.

# TWELVE

"How was your day, William?" William looked up at his dad, who was pouring himself a glass of milk from across the table while keeping his eyes on his plate. Next to him, William's mom devoured her tofu and rain lashed against the sliding glass door in the dining room, with occasional thunder rattling the ceramic tiles that adorned the walls. William stabbed at a piece of overcooked broccoli with his fork, making a few dismal attempts before he managed to spear the vegetable.

"Grand," he answered, eyeing the broccoli with contempt before gulping it down like a carnivorous plant might a fly. "What about you?" William said these words as slowly and audibly as the large vegetable in his mouth would allow, looking somewhat bovine.

"Good," his father answered, staring at his plate once again. "What about you?" he directed his question at William's mom, who was shoveling food off of her plate.

"Good," she said, her mouth full as well. "I was busy today, but one of my students got his acceptance letter from University of Maryland. That was exciting." She began to descend into the details of her day as a high school teacher while William quietly tuned her out and finished his chicken. It was how dinner went, on good and bad days: one question, a few tepid answers and no confrontation, to keep things safe.

"Thank you for dinner," William muttered, jamming the last of his chicken into his mouth as he stood up and gathered his plate, rinsing it off and placing it in the dishwasher while his parents you're-welcomed him. He plodded down the hallway to his room, falling onto his bed and immediately immersing himself in a heavenly array of unmade sheets and pillows, smelling something like a combination of cologne and pop tarts. His tired back settled into the mattress and he let out a sigh of comfort.

His day had sucked and no one had thought twice about it. Not even Leila, it seemed. It was how William had been living lately: wearing a smiling mask to please the people around him, although it only succeeded in covering his own frown. He was something between a therapist and a puppy: used to console but also to gratify, though receiving no fulfillment of his own. He was a prostitute for happiness, without the payment, used for others' satisfaction and then left out to dry.

William instinctively dug his phone out of his pocket and hit his first speed dial number. The name "Olivia Femino" popped up on the cracked screen, and his thumb hit the send button, hearing three rings before a tired voice answered.

"Hey girl, hey," Olivia said from the other line, her scratchy voice making William smile in relief.

"Hey, Olive," he said. "Sorry if it's a bad time. Are you doing anything?"

"Not at all, if you don't include procrastinating," she told him, her voice through the phone sounding like she was much closer than Boise, Idaho. "What's cookin', mediocre-lookin'?" William laughed.

"Thanks, ugly. I don't know," he sighed, content with the satisfaction of talking to someone who would listen. "Today sucked. The whole world, minus a few, thinks I'm a total sleaze because I hooked up with Cassie O'Brien and didn't want to go out with her. Emma threw a bitch fit on me, you're in freaking Idaho, I haven't had a productive conversation with my parents in months, and this girl that I think I like just keeps inviting me into her life and then shutting down again." He caught his breath, realizing that it had run out while he had been talking so rapidly. "Sorry to rant," William added. "I don't like to rant, because it's generally all I hear from other people. I never get a chance to talk, except with you."

Although he hadn't covered every nuance of what upset him,

William felt like he described his current situation fairly well. He had, however, purposefully left out the walks in the dark and the writing and the general feelings of loneliness and disparity that he often felt, instigated by what he felt was nothing. Olivia's best friend had committed suicide two years ago after battling severe depression, and William didn't want to seem like he was faking it, or more importantly, make Olivia talk about it. It was a tender subject to his ex-girlfriend.

"Good grief," Olivia said. Her voice was soothing, despite its abrasive texture. "You need a break from your social life, mister." She meant to continue, but William interceded.

"I have run out of social life juice," he mumbled, tossing a pillow at the wall beside him.

"Shut up," Olivia answered quickly. "You have terrific friends. I have a school full of people who ride their tractors and shit to get to the grocery store. My best friend is my English teacher. Do not complain to me about a giant, gaping void in your social life because mine is bigger. Like my imaginary penis." Before William could comment again, she said, "You need a day off. Eat a lot and watch a soap opera. Let the situation blow over everyone's head and soon enough everyone will love you again."

"Yeah," William answered, mechanically.

"And who is this girl you speak of?" This brought a smile to William's face, as he pictured Leila.

"Leila," he said, into the phone. "The one who draws like a champ." He was grinning as he said this.

Olivia giggled. "The ginger?" she asked, questioning but not criticizing. "She's cute. How do you know her?"

William had to stop himself from telling Olivia about the walking. Leila was the only one who knew.

"Uhh," William closed his eyes and exhaled. "Art class, I guess. I mean, we live in the same neighborhood but we didn't start talking until recently. She's really cool. She has a good taste in music, too. Very Bob Dylan-esque." Though he couldn't see her, William could feel Olivia's smile from the phone, a smile that was thousands of miles away.

"You have my official stamp of approval then, "she said with a laugh, bringing out a grin in William.

They talked for a little over an hour, Olivia talking about herself and William listening as he always did, but this time without a problem. She had gotten a part time job at a local Starbucks, and it was only heightening her loathing for people as a species. Idaho was nice, she told him, but she couldn't adjust. The landscape was scenic and the trees grew more magnificently than they did at home, but Olivia was lonely, longing for her lost best friend and for a busy life with little time to dwell on the past. A question was burning in the back of William's mind, and it would take more courage than he thought he had in him to ask.

"Hey, Olive?" he started, tentatively creeping toward the inquiry in his brain. "Can I ask a personal question? It's okay if you don't want to answer. It's about Erin." William winced, expecting a "no" from Olivia. She wasn't open to questions about her friend's suicide. Instead, he got a static but reliable answer.

"Sure," she replied, her emotions seemingly unchanged, though William could tell that she had stiffened up. Her sure did not sound sure.

"Um," William said, having no choice but to press on with his question. "Did Erin ever hurt herself? Like, before...you know." He grimaced. After the previous night, he had developed growing suspicions about the blood on Leila's left arm. She was right handed and she always wore long sleeves. It was a bold assumption, he knew, but the idea grew in his mind and infected it with each worrying suspicion he had.

Olivia swallowed, and spoke slowly. "Yeah," she said, quietly. "She cut herself for a while, until her parents found out and made her stop. She started throwing up, then. After a while she would just start beating herself. Literally, punching herself all over the place. It was scary. People though it was her parents, so she finally had to admit that she was doing it to herself. She died about a month after she stopped, but there were still a few fading bruises." Olivia sighed. "It's weird what a few fucked up chemicals in your brain can do to your mind and your body."

William was silent, remembering Erin. It was frightening, seeing her so mutilated and broken, and even more frightening to know that she did it to herself. She had a beautiful face, and it was shadowed with bruises that left her cheekbones looking hollow and her eyes looking excruciatingly fatigued, no matter the time of day. Most people cried when the teachers announced Erin's death in eighth grade, but Olivia didn't speak at all. It took almost two weeks for her parents to coerce her into talking again.

"Thanks," William said, "for answering and stuff."

Olivia's voice was slightly muffled from the other end of the phone. "No problem."

A vacuum of silence sucked William up, and he waited for Olivia to speak again.

"I'm going to go," she said, putting on her quiet voice. "I'll text you later."

William nodded to himself. "Okay. You alright?"

"Yeah, bye," Olivia murmured, as if unsure of her answer.

"Bye, Olive." William waited until he heard Olivia hang up, and threw himself back against the pillows, stretching out to his satisfaction. His mind was sore and his body was exhausted, yet he somehow knew that he would not be able to sleep that night. He thought of Olivia often; her dad recovering in rehab and her best friend taking her own life; having to live through another two miserable years of school with people that she hated. Her dreams of going to college in Boston were hanging by a thread, reachable only with a generous scholarship, and she was already working several days a week in a deplorable part-time job.

Olivia had lost so much. Her dad to alcoholism, her best friend to suicide, her home and her aspirations, yet the last thing she would do was pity herself. "When life is tough, you have to be even tougher. Punch that motherfucker in the jaw," she would tell William often. He didn't understand how she remained so positive; William had everything that she had lost, yet she had more faith in the world than he did.

"*Something is horribly wrong with me,*" William thought to himself, inching under the covers as Damian jumped into his bed, laying his head on William's knee. "*I'm unhappy when I should be happy. What am I doing with my life?*" He fumbled for his copy of *The Return of the King*, opening to a random page, letting the paper and the words and the smell of books calm him. He jammed his headphones on and drowned in Bob Dylan. He didn't move for a while, only to turn the pages.

At around nine-thirty, William's mom walked in. "What are you doing, William?" she asked.

"Reading," he answered, sticking a note card with the quadratic formula in the book to mark his page. "What's up?" .

"Nothing," she smiled, placing her hands on her hips with satisfaction. "For the first time in a while, actually. It's nice to do nothing!"

William laughed a little, thinking, "*That is the story of my life, except it's not always nice.*" Both were silent for a few moments, while William's mom gazed around the room complacently.

"I'm not feeling too well," William said, recalling what Olivia had advised him to do. In truth, he was completely worn out, mentally and physically. An off day would do him good.

"What hurts?" his mom asked, walking over to sit at the foot of his bed.

"My stomach," William lied, easily. Years of experience aided him.

"How long has it hurt?" William was forced to lie a little bit more, though he didn't particularly regret it. She left him alone, told him to get plenty of rest and to see how he felt tomorrow morning. He lay his head down and forced his eyes closed, trying to subdue his body into sleeping.

Soon enough, his mind became cloudy and full, with thoughts of Olivia, and Erin's bruised face, Leila's bloody arm, and Emma scowling at him through her rage. The clocked turned from ten to two, each minute crawling idly by while William itched with frustration. He was anxious, and he didn't quite know why, though his brain generated enough ideas for him.

The last time he recalled looking at the clock, it was four fifty-six. His eyelids fell, and he finally slept.

# THIRTEEN

When William awoke to the sound of his alarm the next morning, he promptly began to fake sick. Though he sometimes got migraines, most likely from lack of sleep, William only took days off if he was puking, passed out, or subject to school-induced combustion. Although he didn't have too much experience faking his own sickly condition, it was a capability that most teenagers possessed.

"Mom?" William called, from his bed, receiving no response. "Mom?" None. "Mooommmm?" he half-screeched, half-croaked in an unflattering fashion, hiding himself under the covers as to appear even more tired and weak than he already was. He buried himself in the blankets as she walked in.

"How are you feeling?" she asked him, routinely reaching out to feel his forehead. William forced all of his willpower into making it seem warm.

"Not well," he responded, forcing out a little fake cough. He knew what his mother's next question would be.

"Are you well enough to go to school?"

The fact of the matter was that William simply wasn't, whether it was a matter of physical health or not. He made his face look as pitiful as possible. "I don't think so," he said. "I've got a migraine."

His mom nodded, and crossed her arms. "Okay, go back to sleep then," she told him. "I'll see you this evening. Dad and I will both be home late. Get some rest, drink a lot," and with that she shut William's door after her.

William obeyed every order that Olivia had given him the previous evening; he slept gratefully until noon, when he got up and made himself a bagel. He waddled around the house in sweatpants and watched old episodes of *House*. He caught up on hockey stats and finished part one of *The Return of the King* around four-thirty. Sitting cross-legged on his floor, William pulled an old notebook full of writing out from under his bed, papers flying recklessly from it. He shuffled through old poems, dating back to January 12th, the night with the tree and the bloody snow.

Pulling on his headphones and cuddling up with Squeakers, William began to reread his old writing. Some poems were a bit blasé, and some, frankly, were pointless. He was generally surprised, however, with quite a few things. His words beat nicely, and his vocabulary was shockingly mature. What really caught his eye was a poem he had written shortly after Olivia had moved, and as he read it, he felt his heartstrings twitch.

*They call it goodbye,*
*That one last glance*
*Over the shoulder, eyes filled with longing*
*Wondering, wishing*
*Hoping that you'll see them again*
*They call it goodbye*
*That last, sad hug*
*Holding them tight, tears starting to fall*
*Hoping, pleading*
*Wishing for just one more day*
*They call it goodbye*
*The longing, the sadness*
*Accepting what's happened but not moving on*
*Knowing, holding*
*Saying that you'll never forget*
*Promising that you'll never forget.*

It wasn't particularly original or profound and it lacked the mature word choice that William had developed, but it captured a certain essence that not only made it sound good, but stimulated a certain memory; one that was different for everyone yet almost the same as well. He continued to rummage through the pile, finding not only poems but short stories, song lyrics, other random ramblings that were just like thoughts on paper, only a little more eloquent. He found a note that he had written to Olivia after Erin had died. William had planned on giving it to her, though he never found it in him.

What caught William's eye lay crumpled at the bottom of the pile: a sheet of printer paper with pencil notes scribbled on it, reading, "If your character were to reach into his/her pockets, what would he/she pull out?" This evoked William's curiosity and he picked the paper up, trying to make out the faint, scrawled handwriting. Flipping it over, his brain danced through a beautifully descriptive exposition, titled, "Chapter One." He read through it quickly once, and promptly began to sift through the catastrophic pile of papers that littered his floor. He shuffled through the papers and an occasional article from the *Post*, searching desperately for any additions to this mysterious "Chapter One."

William found his answer at the very bottom of the pile. Four scrawny sheets of loose-leaf paper, each with a small "1" written in the top margin lay in order, detailing the rest of the events of the alleged "Chapter One"; surprisingly well-written prose illustrating a character named Edwin. He was alarmingly average, though he would sometimes sit down at his kitchen and have nice, long talks with his dead uncle, who sometimes showed up for coffee.

His dead uncle, Ross, liked walks on the beach of medium length, as well as people watching; a pastime that he had become quite accustomed to in his experience of being dead. When Ross would leave, Edwin always asked his uncle to take him back to wherever he came from, though Ross' response was always the same, "Not now, buddy. Now ain't a good time for you. Just wait around for a little while."

So Ross would depart and Edwin would continue to be

average and think about being alive and being dead, and being in the gray area in between. He would wonder and wander, more about his own hopelessly mind-numbing future than the fact that his dead uncle stopped by every now and then for coffee.

William read each page through a few times, shocked. He remembered starting this the previous year, though he recalled writing it mostly out of impulse, something resembling a short story rather than a few pages titled "Chapter One." Needless to say, William's mind buzzed. His curiosity neurons connected with his creative nerd cells, splicing through his brain like lightning and he felt an odd, dorky sort of excitement growing in his chest, rising and falling with his pulse.

Standing up with cracking knees, William kicked his pile of unrecognized work back under his bed, keeping with him only the pages that contained "Chapter One," and plodded off toward the den, opposite his bedroom. Barely recognizable beneath Mrs. Spencer's abundance of papers and manila folders, the outlines of a worn-down wooden desk protruded from the mess, housing a mildly-priced laptop that whirred and whispered in its sleep. William sat himself down in the swivel chair across from it and gingerly nudged the machine back to consciousness, opening a blank word document.

William viewed blank word documents the way Leila might, he thought, view a canvas. The keyboard was his paint, and each letter was a different shade of a different color that ultimately created lines and shadows and pictures and memories and art in itself. At the top of the document, centered, William typed, "Chapter Two." He smiled and held his hands above the keys for a few moments, waiting for the words to flood in. When they did, it was like a dam breaking, with letters and sentences and descriptions pouring out and flying from his fingertips, unabated and free. A heavy beat poured from William's headphones, layering on top of the soft but rapid clicking of the keys, each one of equal importance, pounding out each word. He wrote for an hour, and then another, until his ideas dried and the dam closed up again.

Four full pages stared back at him, scrupulously detailed and almost horrifyingly mature and William felt mildly satisfied, though not entirely. He had just written two chapters of something and for some reason that frightened and delighted him at the same time.

It was about six and William heard his mom pull into the driveway through the open den window. Feverishly saving his work to a random desktop folder named "Summer Pics," William dipped from the den and back into his room, launching himself under the covers as his mom walked in the front door, greeted by an energetic Damian and a sleepy Squeakers.

"Will?" she called. He heard her familiar footsteps march into the kitchen and her workbag hit the ground like it always did.

"Yep?" he croaked back.

She walked into William's room, her hair falling out of its ponytail slightly. "Feel any better?"

William nodded. "Yeah. I got some homework done and took a nap and stuff. Hopefully I'll be able to go to school tomorrow."

William *was* able to go to school the next day and for the first time in a while he looked almost human. He said, "Hi," to one person walking into the building, spoke to Anthony in his first period class, answered a few questions in computer science and was otherwise silent for the first half of the day. He skipped lunch once again to hide out in the library and finish some Spanish homework. When he finally made it to art, he walked slowly up to Leila, hoping for some reason that she would ignore him so that he would have some excuse to be mad at her. He wasn't quite sure why he felt that way but she smiled and spoke nonetheless.

"Missed you yesterday," she said, looking up at him for a moment before averting her brown eyes back to the table. "Did you do anything fun, wild or crazy while you were gone?"

William snorted, setting his things down and sitting down

beside her.

"Mainly I took naps and hid from civilization," he said, smoothing his hair down. "It was more of a mental health day. I watched some *House*, ate a couple bagels. Nothing that I wouldn't do on a weekend." He chuckled.

"Any walks?" Leila questioned. William shook his head. They quieted down while Ms. Davis gave a monotonous speech about working and stuff, and Leila seemed to sink back into quietness; something that was okay with her and not with William. He watched her draw for a while. Her hands moved freely, flowing as the contents of her mind poured onto the page in front of her.

"Hey," he started. Leila looked up from her drawing, golden eyebrows slightly arched. "Uh, do you like reading things?" It appeared that Leila didn't quite know what to make of this, and William cursed himself silently.

"It depends on the thing. I read the back of my cereal boxes sometimes. Mostly I read books, though," she said, turning her head back to her work.

William nodded. "Okay, well will you do me a favor?" His decision was impromptu, but the words were out of his mouth, and William couldn't take them back.

"Sure, but I'm not maiming, killing or mentally scarring anyone." Leila was quick in her response.

"Not a problem." William reached into his backpack and pulled out a few sheets of paper; some were furrowed and crumpled, though a few were clean and crisp; neat words on neat printer paper. He folded them up quickly and handed them to Leila. "Can you read these? It's just some writing stuff. A few poems. A short story. I mean you don't have to, but it would be appreciated, and…" William cut himself off.

Leila shrugged, slipping the papers into the back pocket of her grey jeans. "Sure thing. Did you write these?"

"Yeah, it's just some random stuff though. I mean, I just wanted some feedback." William sighed, scratching his head.

Leila just nodded. "Sure, I'll read them later. I'm sure they're grand," she said. "And I really don't mean that in a sarcastic way, sorry. It must have seemed like that."

William chuckled. "A little bit. Thanks, though." He received another nod from Leila, who was deeply immersed in her art. William sighed again, and stared at the adjacent wall until class ended.

# FOURTEEN

The next few days dragged reluctantly and William didn't find himself doing much besides breathing and eating and sometimes learning. When he was at home, he was entirely entwined in his story, finishing what was known as "Chapter Three" by Thursday evening. When sitting in school, he was dreaming up ideas for the alleged "Chapter Four," only engaging in conversations with his teachers, occasionally Anthony and James, and with Leila. When he walked in to art class on Thursday, he asked if she had read what he had written.

She frowned. "Crap, sorry. I totally forgot; I've been swamped with homework. I will, though."

When William asked her on Friday, she pretended to flip the table. "Ugh, I'm sorry. Jeez, I'm the worst," she laughed. "This weekend, I promise."

The weekend passed, and William finished "Chapter Four." He hadn't spoken to Emma since the previous Monday, and had received nothing but dirty looks from Kris, Cassie, and their numerous disciples since then. When, the next day, Leila didn't mention the writing that William had given her the week before, William didn't bother to ask about. It wasn't until Tuesday that she did.

Leila walked into art class about half an hour late, though it didn't appear that Mrs. Davis didn't quite give a damn. She looked exhausted, her bright hair all messy in a bun on the top of her head, black, long sleeves rolled up to her elbows.

"For the love of Lord Stanley, William Spencer," she whispered as she sat down beside him. "Are you actually Charles Dickens or something? That stuff that you wrote was incredible."

William snorted, though it appeared that Leila was saying this in all seriousness.

"Do you have more?"

"Leila, William," Mrs. Davis started, looking up from her desk. "Shut your mouths."

William giggled.

"Yeah, much more," he admitted. He was going to tell her about chapters two through four, but she beat him to it.

"I love Ross. Seriously, he is one of my favorite characters in any piece of literature ever. I like him as much as I liked Death in *The Book Thief*. He's literally a genius, are you aware of that?" William scratched his head.

"I wasn't, not really," he admitted, in all honesty. "He's just kind of chilling, being dead and all."

"Ugh, he's just so..." Leila searched for words, ending up defeated. "He's great. I wish he was my uncle."

"Leila!" Mrs. Davis snapped from the front of the room. "I don't care how talented you are. Art comes from your hands, not your mouth."

Leila shook her head. "Totally false," she said, only to be ignored again by Mrs. Davis.

"Music is art. Music comes from people's mouths, doesn't it? Bob Dylan made art with his mouth. And his lungs and maybe his esophagus and stuff, but still," Leila huffed. "The mouth is the apparatus for art."

William chuckled, nodding along compliantly. "You tell 'em," he grinned, slightly sarcastic. Leila just rolled her eyes.

William was glad for Mrs. Davis for once, seeing as she had diverged Leila's train of thought, along with her endless stream of slightly embarrassing compliments. Receiving praise was awkward for him; though he appreciated it fully, he never quite knew how to respond.

"Hey," William started, wanting just to speak to Leila more than anything else. All ideas for conversation in his head were null, and he panicked. "Spring break is the end of this week, right?" In his mind, William was saying, *"William Spencer, you are a moron."*

Leila seemed to find no fault with this, however, and smiled excitedly. "Yes indeed. "We just have this week, and then we're off. Doing anything fun?"

William shook his head. "Nope," he sighed, "I will just sit on my butt and maybe take some naps." He stifled a laugh. "Spring break isn't that different from my life now, I just find that I get to sleep a little more."

Leila only nodded sympathetically. "Understandable. I don't think my plans are too different." She laughed. "Although, I'm fairly excited for the sleeping part."

William nodded, shuffling through words in his head. Writing and speaking were two totally different concepts to him; he was eloquent on paper, but clumsy otherwise. Words would formulate in his mind, but they couldn't find their way out of his mouth.

"We should, um," he stumbled. "Hang out." Pause, smile, shame. William cursed his inability to speak normally, though was wholly relieved when Leila smiled.

"I agree," she answered. "Though, maybe during the daytime. I'm really not some sort of monster who bursts into flames upon contact with sunlight."

William laughed. "That sucks, because I am," he joked.

"Bummer."

William tried to remember the last time he had made plans to hang out with someone other than Emma. He had gone to James' bonfire, but that was a rarity; he hardly went to parties. There was that rendezvous with Cassie, but that was undesirable anyway. He had been quite the social butterfly all throughout middle school, and even as a freshman, though when sophomore year rolled around he began to quiet down. He turned down offers to hang out and instead spent his time reading Dante's 'Inferno' or watching soap operas. As a result of the past week, he could list on one hand the people he would call his friends.

William couldn't help but wonder why Leila seemed so alone

at times. She was amicable and funny despite her generally reserved attitude and she made William feel honestly good. She would be well liked if she was well known. Then again, maybe she simply chose not to be.

"Can I ask you something?" he blurted out.

Leila shrugged. "You just did." She smirked behind delicate eyelashes as William rolled his eyes.

"Ha. But in all seriousness, it's a serious question," he admitted. "That was redundant. But..." a sigh escaped his lips, and he closed his eyes, "what's on your arm?"

Leila shrugged again, looking at the table. "Skin."

"That's not what I mean," William said softly. "You've got scratches, or cuts, or something on your left arm. I'm not really sure, but I'm concerned and stuff."

Leila looked straight ahead, her eyes locked on nothing except the molecules floating about in the air. Her mouth twitched slightly and she remained silent.

"We don't have to talk about it," William began, before Leila quickly interrupted him.

"Let's not, then, please," she said quickly, tugging on her hair. William nodded.

"Alright, we won't," he said. "But if you ever want to, we can. You seem like you've got a lot to say."

"I do," Leila bit her lip. "I just don't know how or when to say it." She looked at him with wide eyes. "Just don't worry about me; I can take care of myself. I know when to draw the line. I already trust you not to tell anyone. Don't worry about me," she repeated, turning her head back to the table so that a section of red hair hid her whitening face.

William felt his heart drop like a rock into his unsuspecting tummy.

"But, isn't it nice to vent sometimes?" he inquired, oozing with empathy.

Leila, however, shook her head. "Not to people. They either

judge or don't care, and the ones who do," she stopped to think. "I just feel bad. I don't want to burden them. I hate when people worry about me."

William could only think to nod. He felt like he understood, but at the same time he couldn't.

"Alright," he said, admitting defeat. "But if you want to talk or anything, just let me know."

"Thanks," Leila said, obviously embarrassed. "I'd prefer to be distracted, actually. Just so I can think about other things. Keep my mind elsewhere."

"I can, uh, tell you about Ross..." William's mind was reeling, tossing and turning with thoughts of Leila and her arms and even of Erin and her self-destructive ways. "And his backstory and stuff, if you want."

Leila shrugged. "Okay."

William told Leila about Ross, a story that he had sort of come up with earlier but was making impromptu additions to. All the while she sat quietly, occasionally sketching a few things onto her portrait only to erase them again, not uttering a word. William realized, with the growing development of his story, that Ross' life had a frightening resemblance to his. When Ross should have been happy, he wasn't. When Ross should have felt content, he was nervous. Nervous about anything, whether something bad was to happen the next day or within the year, Ross never got over his constant anxiety.

It reminded William of himself, and it scared him.

I like Ross," Leila stated again, out of the blue. "I like that I can relate to him."

William suddenly swore that Leila could read his thoughts. "Yeah, me too."

The end of the period rolled around and with a few minutes to go, Leila picked a pen off the table and held her hand out. "Let me see your arm," she said.

William raised an eyebrow, cautiously placing his right arm

in her hand. Without looking up at him, Leila scribbled a number across his forearm.

"Hit me up, or something. We should hang out. You're pretty cool." The bell rang then and Leila got up without another word, her red hair bouncing with her careful steps.

William glanced at his arm, looked at Leila exiting the room, looked back at his arm. He looked at his arm on his way to Spanish class, reading the number over and over again. He doodled trees and street lamps and houses around it in blue and black pens until his arm had grown into one of Leila's brilliant canvases, though not as impressive. He didn't speak until the end of the day, when Emma walked up to him, Batman converse and curly hair standing out against her skin.

"Hey," she started. William looked up from his arm, nodding in her direction. His mind detached itself from the phone number and he began to wonder why Emma was bothering to talk to him in the first place. It took him a moment to realize that she was once his best friend, or something along those lines.

"Hey, Emma," he said, rolling down the sleeves of his gray hoodie. "What's up?"

Emma surveyed the ground, fidgeting her right leg. Her hands were buried deep in the pockets of her jeans and her shoulders hunched up around her ears, making her look uncharacteristically uncomfortable. She sighed, her mouth twitching slightly to one side.

"Not much," she said, meeting his gaze for only a moment, her blue eyes flickering around nervously. "How have you been?"

William only shrugged. "Fine," he said. *"Fine, since you burned every bridge I had ever toiled over to build,"* he thought. "Yeah, I've been well. You?"

She nodded. "I've been good," she said, tugging at the ends of her hair. Both were silent and William looked at her expectantly. "Um." She bit her lips, all the nervous signs combining to make

William uncomfortable as well. "I think I just want to say sorry for being a huge dick to you, and stuff. I shouldn't have said those things. It was inconsiderate."

William raised his eyebrows. His natural instinct was to buckle down and smile, to say it was okay and wave off their faults. With his newly grown backbone, William fought this off.

"Yeah, it was," he said, finally locking eyes with her. He remained emotionless, while she looked just about to break down. In all of his life, William could only remember seeing Emma cry once, when Erin died. "Sorry if I said anything bad, too," he said. He wanted to apologize for making her angry in the first place, but he stopped himself. His mission was to be assertive.

Frankly, the bell saved his ass. Before Emma could say anything, he stood up, slinging his backpack over his shoulder. "I'll see you later, Emma," he said, smiling at her baffled expression. He walked out into the sun.

# FIFTEEN

On the last Thursday before spring break was to start, William forfeited his Spanish homework to write, transitioning from Thursday night into Friday morning. When he finished writing around two-thirty, he had a large headache and a fifth chapter to show Leila. It was the first time he had stayed up so late without walking. William found Leila before school started that Friday, sitting outside of the band room with her headphones in, quickly scribbling some English homework. His soul began to float about in her lightly perfumed smell.

"Hey," she said, looking up with eyes lightly brushed with makeup. Her sunset hair was faintly wavy with frizz toward the ends and her grey jeans swung with the slight curve of her hips. She wore a black sweater that covered most of the peach tank top below it; only allowing a few pastel-colored glances to peek through.

"Hey," William handed her the newest chapter, four pages stapled unevenly and creased across the front from being stuffed into his backpack. Leila perked up suddenly and snatched it out of his hands with a smile, dropping her homework without hesitation. "I brought you the story," William said, rather blatantly, suddenly empty handed while Leila began to read.

She nodded her head, eyes locked upon the page. "Did you, now?"

Her dry humor brought a smile to William's lips. "Yeah," he admitted, smoothing down a few auburn strands that were peeking up from his scalp. "Don't get too excited, I'm not about to write you a chapter every day."

Leila shot him a look. "You better, though," she said, standing up.

William didn't realize until right then that she was almost his height, making it easy for him to count all the colors in her eyes.

"You can't just leave me on a cliffhanger or anything. This book has quickly become my favorite book."

William chuckled a little, alarmed however to see that Leila looked genuinely serious.

"Really, it isn't that good," he said, honestly. "And it's not a book. I'm not even fishing for compliments or anything. Like, I just started writing it out of impulse. I don't have a storyline drawn out or character sketches or anything." He sighed a little, blowing out a thin stream of air. "As much as I would love to have it finished at some point, there is an astronomically thin chance of that actually happening." The bell rang then, and Leila put her hand on William's back, guiding him down the hallway.

"You will finish this book, William, because I demand it," she said, sternly but with a grin. "You will finish it before we graduate and then send it in for publication. You will get to describe the writing process in all of your college essays and get this motherfucker in the bookstores."

William cracked a smile, hearing the way she had said "we."

Two days before, he had spent at least twenty minutes staring at the phone number scribbled on his arm, contemplating exactly how to put it into his phone. He kept continuously scrolling through his contacts, just to see Leila's name. He creeped himself out at times.

"Besides," she added, dropping her hand as she darted around a few people blocking the hallway, "If you need character sketches, I would be delighted to do them for you. Ross is mixed, his dad is white and his mom is African American. He has a little bit of scruff, but not enough to call it a beard or anything. He dresses well and he has a nice singing voice, and he keeps a ring of keys in his pocket, but I'm not sure why. You described him in chapter two."

"Girl." William smiled. "Can I recruit you? Your memory is better than mine. I can't even remember writing that."

Leila shrugged. "As long as you don't call me that." She

brushed her hair out of her eyes. William noticed that her hands were almost as big as his. He nodded, approaching Mr. Monroe's room. "Sure thing," he said. "Hey, I'll see you in fifth. Read the chapter."

"Cool, I will. See you," she said, patting him on the shoulder.

William watched her walk away, waving affably to one of her friends. He smiled and walked into his classroom, setting his bag down gently beside his desk. The room was rather empty, with the exception of Mr. Monroe and a girl named Angelica, so William took the opportunity to take an old notebook from his backpack and scribble the words "Chapter Six," across the margin of the first sheet of paper. His writing flow had hit a barrier, but it was beginning to break through.

After the late bell rang and William listened to a few generic announcements about some talent shows and a dance concert, Mr. Monroe passed out what looked like an essay rubric.

"We're starting our creative writing unit today, folks," he said, pacing back and forth.

William perked up, an apparent contrast to Anthony, who was napping.

"Your assignment," he continued, shuffling through a stack of papers on his desk, "is to write me a short story based around a general theme of adventure. I want elements of romance; knights, chivalry, magic, corny stuff like that. Think *The Princess Bride*."

*The Princess Bride*, what William thought was a literary and satirical masterpiece, was one of the first books his English class had read that year. It took more than a month for the class to stop saying, "Hello, my name is Inigo Montoya. You killed my father. Prepare to die!"

"Don't take this assignment too lightly," Mr. Monroe went on, sitting cross-legged on his desk beneath one of the many paper lanterns that hung about his room. "I'm expecting anywhere from four to eight pages. Two hundred points." The class groaned at this, but William smiled to himself. "Shut up," Mr.

Monroe said. "Write me a novel if you wish. I'm looking for a protagonist on a lofty quest. It can be the search for the Holy Grail, or it can be a search for his or her purpose in life. Medieval England or Massachusetts, in 1776. I'm giving you a lot of leeway here, guys."

"When will this be due?" a girl in the front of the class asked.

"Whenever I want it to be," Mr. Monroe answered without hesitation. "Since you all seem so keen' on doing every assignment the night before it's due anyway."

Anthony picked up his head. "So, you're not going to tell us when it's due?" he asked, like Mr. Monroe was stupid. The English teacher smiled, scratching his chin.

"Oh, I'll tell you the day before," he said, with a wry grin. "Better get working on it soon then, Anthony, if you plan on getting any more sleep." Anthony rolled his eyes. The class slowly shifted into a discussion about dystopian societies, and William found himself drifting back into his mind, thinking of nothing but Edwin and Ross and how they would fit nicely into his short story.

The rest of the day was spent counting down the hours until fifth period. No one mentioned Cassie to him, and he was able to make normal conversation with most people, though he was still cautious. He went to lunch for once and though he got a few evil glares thrown his way, he still managed to have an enjoyable and rather social time.

Though William spent the most of journalism in solitude, he greeted Emma on his way in, and said goodbye on his way out. He could tell by the way that she looked at him with her blue eyes and her lips slightly parted that she had much to say to him, she had simply decided against it. It was almost delightful.

At 12:15, William promptly left for the art room, walking into the deepening aroma of charcoal, pastels and paint. He spotted Leila sitting in her usual spot at the back table, her eyes cast down at a few stapled pages. William smiled wryly as he sat down next to her.

"Not finished yet?" he asked. She blinked, but appeared unfazed.

"Sorry," she said, not sounding very sorry. "I didn't have much time today. Anderson's been killing us with AP test reviews. He expects no less than a four from just about everyone."

William nodded sympathetically, silently thanking himself for not taking AP government.

"Jennifer's kind of a douche," she said, looking up from the pages on the table.

William grinned. Jennifer was Edwin's lifelong companion, who had recently grown self-centered and condescending.

"She's not really that bad." He shrugged, thinking of Emma, remembering their countless days that went from Pitt's to the pond and then off to some unknown destination, crossing their seemingly endless Maryland county all for the sake of exploring. He felt guilty, against what seemed like his better judgment.

Leila cocked her head to the side and gave him an unfazed smile. "I'm not a huge fan." She shrugged. "Every story needs its douchebags though, right?"

William nodded. "I suppose so. Just like life, huh?" He elbowed her.

"Are you trying to tell me that I am the douchebag in your life?" she asked, elbowing him back much harder. William meant to tell her just the opposite but was silenced by Mrs. Davis and the clicking of her high-heels.

"Mr. Spencer, if I catch you flirting with Leila in my class one more time, I might actually hit you," she snapped, eyes trained on the ground as usual. A few students giggled, and William felt heat crowd his face, his cheeks no doubt turning bright red. Leila rolled her eyes, shrinking back into her seat while Mrs. Davis continued.

"Today," she started, "you will do work. Or you will be

someone who chooses not to do work." Her voice sounded harsh, like grass being ripped from the ground. "In that case, your grade will suffer. And then your life will suffer. Clear?" Most of the class sniggered. "Good. Go work."

Leila started to get up, but William rushed ahead of her. "Hey, I got you," he said. He found her portrait, along with his weak effort of a painting, and gathered their materials. Though he wouldn't admit it, he was remembering something that Kris had told him months ago.

"Bitches love chivalry."

It seemed like a joke coming from Kris, but William could only suppose that it was true. He walked back to the table with his arms full, setting down the paintings and materials, to see a male face sitting in his seat. Nathan, a freshman who he had never really gotten to know, sat beside Leila, wearing a smug grin as they made casual conversation. She laughed as he whispered something in her ear, and William felt his stomach tighten. An anvil had just fallen.

"Oh, hey," Nathan said, smiling. "Sorry. Took your seat." He stood up and offered the stool back to William.

"No problem." William sat, his eyes trained on Nathan, who walked casually back to his seat. "Who's that?" he asked, although he already knew.

"Nathan Armstead," Leila replied, reaching for a paintbrush. "What of it?"

William shrugged, defensively. "Nothing. Curious," he lied. He tried to remember any little chunks of knowledge about Nathan that might have been hiding in the back of his mind. He found one. "Wait, didn't he set a bathroom on fire in middle school? I swear I heard that about him."

Leila snorted. "Yeah."

William gaped, dumbfounded. "What, wait, how?" He raised his eyebrows. "How did he even go about doing that?"

Leila shook her head, laughing. "I don't know, ask him," she suggested, motioning to where he was sitting with a few other freshman. "Are you planning on setting a bathroom on fire?"

William shook his head. "No, I just think it's weird," he admitted, rolling up his sleeves. "I didn't think you'd be so eager to befriend one who sets bathrooms on fire." William knew immediately that the words that were coming out of his mouth were the wrong ones, but he couldn't stop them. It was like trying to stop swallowing water when you had already started. He braced himself.

"And what are you implying?" Leila furrowed her delicate eyebrows, not sounding particularly angry just rather annoyed. "You're judging Nathan based off of something he did two years ago. You don't even know him. I'll be friends with whomever I please, if you don't mind." She crossed her arms, defensively.

The first word that came to William's mind was 'eloquent.' Instinctively, he put his hands up in a gesture of surrender. "Sorry," he said. "I'm not trying to insult you or him or anything. I'm purely curious."

"I can talk to other people, you know," she said, not meaning for it to sound as patronizing as it did.

William nodded sarcastically as she turned her eyes down to her self-portrait.

"Right. I wasn't implying that you couldn't," he said, in his own justification. "I was just...yeah. Whatever, let's drop it, please," he huffed, turning his eyes down, though Leila's face lit up slightly with a grin.

"Sure," she concurred. "Do your work."

William shook the argument out of his head and turned instead to his self-portrait, which lay half-finished on the table. A spark lit in his brain, turning to a flame and growing larger and larger as he touched a piece of charcoal to the paper, outlining the shape of a road winding across his face and weaving through his hair. Headlights glared out of the darkness; two menacing, blinding eyes that meant that his secrets were no longer safe.

Trees, standing on guard to protect him from drug dealers and rabid possums. Red leaves fell.

"Hey," Leila whispered, prodding William in the side. He looked up to see her holding out one of her headphones to him. The sound of soft guitar strings floated out. William smiled, and took it graciously, putting it into his ear and losing himself in a word of acoustics and folk music.

# SIXTEEN

William began to pack up relatively early, carefully picking up his portrait and placing it back on the drying rack. He stood in front of it for a moment, silently admiring the painting he was creating. Upon first receiving the assignment William had planned to add a few random symbols of birds or stars that happened to mean nothing to him and make it seem like he was really passionate about self-portraits. He didn't actually expect himself to become so engrossed in his own artwork.

Leila appeared on William's left. "Lookin' good," she said, stepping toward the sink to wash off a few paint brushes, the color running down her fingers with the steaming water as she squeezed the bristles gently.

William realized that she was talking about his painting. "Thanks," he responded, scratching the back of his head with the hand that wasn't covered in paint. "It's just kind of random."

"You sure about that?" Leila smirked, drying her brushes off with a paper towel and placing them tenderly into their designated drawer. "Midnight meander...ers," she whispered, putting her arm through the crook of his elbow and leading him back to their table.

"Hey," William started, blindly navigating his butt onto the stool so as to maintain eye contact with Leila. He sat. "You trying to hang out over break? Like, at a normal time of day." He saw her smile, rolling her brown eyes playfully.

"Of course," she responded, zipping up her backpack. It was faded blue, with words written in metallic sharpie. "*All the truth in the world adds up to one big lie.*"

"I'm free at any day at any time, besides Sundays. I can't really do anything on Sundays ever." Leila continued. William asked why not. "I have voice lessons," she told him.

William raised his left eyebrow. "You sing?" he asked.

"You breathe?" she challenged. William shrugged, agreeing that she made a valid point. It would be the same if someone had asked him about writing.

"I just didn't know," he admitted. "I haven't heard you."

Leila smiled. "Come to a choir concert and you will. I've had a few solos."

Though he knew she hadn't meant to sound offensive or condescending, William couldn't help but feel guilty. She didn't seem, at first glance, like the type to sing for a crowd, but inside he knew she had the confidence to do so. He asked the question that all musicians hated. "Are you good?"

"Fabulous," she smirked. "On a scale from one to Adele, I'm a twelve."

William shrugged. "I'll assume you're pretty good, in that case."

The bell rang, and William hung around for a minute while Leila put her things away. She stood up and kicked her stool under the table, swinging the blue backpack with the silver sharpie letters over one shoulder. Her arms, blanketed in long sleeves, held the door for him as he walked out.

*"Bitches love chivalry,"* William thought and laughed to himself.

"What?" Leila asked, speeding up a bit to walk beside him. William shook his head. Leila began to depart for a different hallway, a voice like saccharine stopped her. Cassie, dressed down in yoga pants and a normal, unhampered T-shirt, bounced to Leila's side, giving her a wide smile as she brushed wordlessly past a skeptical, sour-faced boy named William, who stopped in the middle of the hall and glared.

"Hey, girl!" she chirped. "I *love* your hair today." Cassie threw Leila a thousand-watt smile, casting a fleeting glance over toward a frowning William. "So, uh, I heard you saying that you were having trouble in Morrison's class, and I was wondering if you wanted any help. I'm not too bad at precalc." She laughed a little, each sound wave mocking William, flashing the word "anger" in giant red letters before his eyes. He hoped that some otherworldly force would snap inside of Leila, causing her to land a right hook to Cassie's jaw, though he found himself disappointed.

Leila pitched William a subtle glance, quick enough to prevent Cassie from seeing, but long enough to ensure that William knew she was just as alarmed. "Uh, I'm not really having much trouble in that class anymore, actually," she responded, awkwardly trying to match Cassie's enthusiastic smile. "But, you know, I can always let you know if I am."

Cassie's smile wavered for a second. "Oh." She raised her eyebrows. "Been getting help from Will?" She didn't look at him when she said it, but her tone of voice carried enough disdain to kill a grown bear.

"No," Leila said, unfalteringly.

William, however, shot lasers through the back of Cassie's head.

"You've been spending a lot of time with him." Cassie shrugged, crossing her arms. "I mean, there's nothing wrong with that. I just wouldn't recommend it. He's sort of a dick to girls that he pretends to like."

Both William and Leila stared with the same disbelieving expression. "Well," Leila began, "I'll, uh, look out for him? I guess. Thanks." She shot William one more glance before she walked down the hall, leaving Cassie looking slightly perturbed. William walked past her, stopping only for a moment to stand in front of her.

"You're cool," he said, blankly, walking in the opposite direction before she could say a word. His breathing grew more stressed and with each step he resisted the escalating urge to hit the wall next to him where he though its face would be.

Of course Cassie was targeting Leila, he thought. Of course she would want to reveal all of the dirt on his high school soul so as to keep Leila away from him. She was sly, but she had all intent of ruining him; she was a covert beast beneath her sweet appearance. The bell rang again, though he didn't bother rushing through the hallways.

He stormed into Spanish class, slamming the door behind him to the alarm of his class, particularly Emma, who was hiding a pair of headphones in the sleeve of her sweatshirt.

"Why are you late, Will?" His Spanish teacher's monotonous voice filled his head. William sat.

"Sorry," he replied, keeping his eyes down. "I don't really want to talk about it." He expected detention or a lecture on timeliness or something else teacher-y, but he only received a look of sympathy, and a quiet, "llueges a tiempo manana, por favor."

William nodded compliantly and set to work conjugating verbs to the present perfect tense. He scribbled angrily, though the irritated scratches from his chewed-up pencil were null beneath the quiet hum of voices in the classroom.

Frustration pulsed through his veins, throbbing and beating and threatening to explode out of his body in a grand spectacle. He had done Cassie one thing wrong and she retaliated with a force ten times greater, bringing him embarrassment, disapproval and, most significantly, unforgiving solitude. For the damage he had done to her, she reciprocated harder and more detrimentally, leaving him stripped of his dignity.

William fidgeted nervously upon remembering Cassie's interaction with Leila, who had somehow managed to see William's misgivings. He wondered silently if Cassie had prompted Leila to change her mind.

"Will," a scratchy voice whispered to him, followed by the feeling of a pencil smacking the back of his head. He turned to see Emma and her Star Wars T-shirt staring at him, her blue eyes searching every crevice and lifeline of his face. This time, it was William who looked angry.

"What?" he hissed, averting his gaze immediately. He could only fathom how red his face might be. Emma didn't back off, though she lowered her voice slightly.

"Don't get too sassy there, captain," she said, reiterating a phrase that William used to hear frequently. "I just wanted to ask if you're okay."

William didn't look at her, just scratched the back of his head, exhaling deeply. "Fuckin' grand, why do you ask?" he muttered, catching her gaze by accident. She held it.

"You're literally tapping the hell out of your desk with your pencil," Emma said, nonchalantly. "If you keep that up, I will flip something." They both shared a stifled laugh, which William tried hard to suppress.

"Yeah, well," William shrugged, putting his skeptical face back on. "I'm just tapping." Emma's expression was unfazed.

"Also, you were late," she retaliated. "And you didn't want to talk about it and you just look grumpy so something is up."

William nodded, wearing a sour, sarcastic expression. "Well done. You have me all figured out," he said, in a monotone. From behind himself, William could hear Emma sigh exasperatedly, before he felt her grab a hunk of his tousled hair and yank him back toward her, painfully. "Ow, fuck. Ow. Emma, stop it, good grief."

Emma released her death grip on William's hair once he was turned around and within a two foot vicinity of her. "Listen," she whispered, not particularly angrily but with enough authority to snap him to attention. "I apologize." William sighed as Emma tried desperately to keep his attention. "I know I'm not the *best* best friend out there. I can be a handful. I just get incredibly passionate about things and defensive and you know that, but I'm still sorry for being ridiculous. I should have tried to be more tolerant, but I just snapped at you that day in journalism and I was too big-headed to admit that I wasn't right."

William blinked. "Are you *actually* apologizing first?" he

inquired.

"Don't mock me," Emma said, although a faint smile was beginning to spread across her face. "You were right, that's all, and I'm obviously not a big fan of admitting that I'm wrong. Even if I am, I just continue to argue as if I'm right. I am accepting defeat," she admitted, with a shrug.

William purposefully gaped, looking as astounded as possible, causing Emma to laugh her hiccupy laugh and smack him lightly upside the head.

"That shit cray," William exclaimed in his best whisper-yell, smacking Emma back. They attempted to glare at one another, though they each erupted into giggles momentarily.

"I know," she said. "I just figured I'm pretty lame by myself. Be my best friend again?" William smiled, though he held in an immediate answer.

"I'll have to sleep on that one," he said. "Meanwhile, though, I'll get you the best friend contract. You have a lot of paperwork to fill out." William's delighted smile bathed his whole face in bliss.

"Ugh, William!" Emma groaned. "Just cooperate with me, here."

William laughed, shaking his head. "I'm kidding. I never stopped being your best friend, dummy." He grinned. "However, it appears that Mr. Martini is glaring at me, and I already came in late. So walk home with me? We'll talk then, wench." He gave her a quick salute and scooted his chair back to the appropriate desk.

"Alright, wench, Emma replied with a pleased expression.

An elephant had just walked out of the room, carrying the enormous weight that had previously been chilling on William's chest and he found himself feeling rather peaceful and content. He paid attention, a task which was both difficult for him and not often completed, thinking about Spanish and about his best friend. Thoughts of Cassie and Leila and even Kris tried to worm their way into his mind but he pushed them out with ease, thinking, "You are not welcome here, bad or nerve-inducing thoughts. You must go now."

They went.

# SEVENTEEN

Every cell in William's body stood at attention, alert but calm, as he walked out of school with Emma, feeling humble and rejuvenated. The sky was overcast and grey, tiny drops of rain embracing the sidewalk as they elegantly tumbled down from infinity. Students ducked in and out of the building, running to their buses or to someone's nearby umbrella in order to protect their hair or their books or their phones. William took a deep breath in.

"Quit dawdling, wench, I'm getting wet," Emma whined, frantically smoothing down her hopelessly frizzy hair.

William laughed. "Your hair can look good any other day. Just take a minute to enjoy the rain. It's just so...miraculous." It took him a few seconds of gazing up at the sky to notice Emma's skeptical expression, one hand placed on the deep curve of her hip with authority.

"Yeah, we're going to enjoy it the whole way home!" she exclaimed, though it was easy to tell she wasn't entirely displeased. "It rains all the time, anyway, what's so special about this time?"

William shrugged, taking her arm and leading her away from the main entrance of Hawthorne River; over towards the tennis courts, the back field and the little path they would take home.

"Rain should be special all the time, don't you think? Like, in some places, it rains for months, and then disappears. We take it for granted, don't you think? What if we didn't have rain? It's a miracle." He smiled, ruffling Emma's hair with his fist. "Besides, I'm always here to mess up your hair."

"And I'm here to mess up the bone structure in your face when you do!"

They grinned at one another, paying little attention to the confused, condescending stares of their peers. If anything, they made William feel better, assuring him of the fact that people knew he would always have a friend in Emma, somewhere deep inside her damaging comebacks and ever-present wit. Rumors would tear William from his class and his school and the walls of safety that he had set up around himself, but they couldn't tear him from his best friend.

"So, captain, why were you sufficiently displeased during Spanish class today?" Emma asked, holding her backpack over her head in an attempt to stay dry. "I thought you were going to, like, flip a desk or something.

William heaved a sigh, trudging through the dampening grass and mud of the giant, emerald green field behind Hawthorne River. "Well, you know how I've been hanging out with Leila a lot?" he inquired, his stomach dropping like an anvil upon mentioning her name. Though he was comfortable with Leila herself, he still wasn't quite used to talking about her. He felt that words couldn't do her justice.

"The ginger. Right," Emma agreed, stepping over a puddle with precision. "Do you like her?"

"I don't know." William waited for a sassy remark about making up his mind, but Emma only shrugged. "Anyway," he continued, "Cassie just randomly started talking to her after art today. She was trying to, like, warn her about how horrible I was to girls that I liked, or something. It's bullshit. I didn't even like her. We barely talked!" he huffed, marching irately.

"You don't actually think Leila would believe that though, do you?" Emma asked, squinting her left eye as the rain beat its fists upon them.

William looked at her, silently asking her to elaborate.

"I mean, she never flipped out on you when the whole Cassie thing exploded, right?" Emma continued, taking refuge beneath her backpack again.

William shrugged. "Well, no. But she probably–" He was interrupted by Emma's shushing.

"Leila's pretty shy and she opened up to you fairly quickly, didn't she?"

Her words prompted a flashback of the school parking lot and the dark world in William's mind; the first time he had really seen Leila in every fine detail of her personality.

"I'm pretty ninety-seven percent sure that she doesn't talk to Cassie too often, so why would she believe Cassie over you?"

William looked puzzled. "I don't know, maybe it's a girl thing?" he suggested, phrasing it as more of a question than a statement.

Emma rolled her eyes as she and William emerged from the back field and stepped onto the bike path that led to their homes, shaded by the overhanging branches of curious trees.

"That's a common misconception, you see," she said, mocking William in her most scholarly voice. "It doesn't matter if they're both girls or whatever. They're totally different, if you haven't noticed and Cassie hasn't exactly given Leila a reason to trust her."

"How do you know that *I* have?" William asked, reaching up to brush a few leaves with his fingertips.

"I can tell."

He decided that this was sufficient answer and pushed the thought out of his mind.

As they walked on through the rain, Emma told William about her interactions with Alex, the boy he knew she had feelings for. She regaled him with news of Randy and Dan the Van, whose driver's seat window recently stopped working.

It was strange, William figured, to be catching up with someone who you had only gone a few days without speaking to. The damage was greater though, he supposed, when the absence was that of a best friend. Any silence between himself and Emma was almost unbearable. He was glad for Emma's resilience; that she would accept his friendship again with no questions asked.

They parted at their usual spot behind William's house without any excessive celebration; no hugging or handshaking or statements of, "Hey, I'm glad we're best friends again."

They simply said goodbye and promised to hang out over spring break, though they made it a point to avoid bonfires at all costs. William waved to Emma once more as he scampered across his mud-soaked back lawn, little estuaries of water trickling down the gently sloping grass. He sped to the porch and yanked the back door open to be greeted by dry air, as well as Damian and Squeakers, both of whom smelled atrocious.

"Hey, boys," he spoke in a childlike voice, dropping his backpack and kneeling down to pet his over-excited dogs. Their tails wagged gale-force winds, pink tongues hanging lazily from the corners of their mouths.

They followed him excitedly up the stairs, where he was greeted by his mom, who stood in the hallway with her workbag, brushing her hair quickly, an apple held between her teeth.

"Hi, Weeyum," she said, the apple obstructing the path from her voice box to her mouth. "Oops. Hi, William," his mother said again, taking the apple from her mouth and dropping it indifferently into her bag. "I have to go back to work," she told him, placing a hand on William's shoulder as she inched past him. "I'll be home late. There are TV dinners in the freezer. Dad should be home around six, okay?"

William's mom didn't wait for a response, just smiled and kissed his cheek. As she headed towards the front door, pausing to slip on her shoes, William called, "Hey, mom?"

"Yeah?"

He looked at her, her slightly frizzy hair, an aging yet tender face, smoothed over with signs of prosperity, attentive eyes and "experience lines." She wouldn't call them wrinkles.

"You work too much," he told her, finally. They exchanged bittersweet smiles, before she said goodbye and headed out the door.

William stood alone for a few moments, hearing the hum of her hybrid car start up and then dissipate down the street. Walking into the kitchen with Damian and Squeakers at his heels, he inhaled the natural scent of rosemary, a few leaves lying on the counter, picked fresh from the garden. NPR, like an old friend, filled his ears with familiar voices.

William grabbed a bowl and a box of Cheerios from the cabinets above the kitchen sink and sat at the counter, that day's edition of *The Washington Post* sitting idly in front of him, open to page A4. He poured himself some cereal, sitting back in his chair while news from the nation's capital enveloped him and swam to his brain.

His faithful dogs curled up beneath him, tails smacking the ground in earnest, creating a sporadic rhythm that rivaled the steady sound of the radio. As he ate, William thought about his mom, and how it was Friday, and how she deserved a proper Shabbat for once. The more he thought about this, the more he began to think about his heritage and his religion; how he was so proud of his Judaism, yet he hardly knew anything about it.

William was spiritual; he would pray and he believed in God, but he often felt himself to be inadequate. He couldn't speak Hebrew and he didn't know the Torah and he was a Hebrew School dropout. He began to delve deep inside himself, realizing how badly he felt about not having a Bar Mitzvah and how he ate bacon frequently. His faith was an aspect of his life that he took for granted, and he hated himself for it.

Taking a few last bites of his cereal, William sprang up suddenly, an idea developing in his mind. He put his bowl away in the dishwasher hurriedly, hastening down the hallway to his room, Damian following him in earnest as he pushed open his door while Squeakers remained in the kitchen, sniffing around for any Cheerios that may have been dropped.

William tore through the mess in his room and knelt down beside his bookcase, shuffling through copies of his favorite young adult novels, classics and epics and his old collection of *TinTin* comic books. He was powered entirely by one image: that of a white hardback picture book. It was found on the bottom shelf, hiding between *The Gift of the Magi* and a Webster's Dictionary, its top covered in a thin layer of dust.

He pulled out his illustrated Jewish children's bible, his eyes scanning the front cover and analyzing every detail from the author's name to the drawing of Moses, whose hands stretched outwards as thunderclouds accumulated around his glorious being. Taking a deep breath, William opened the first page, scanning the table of contents and reading the introduction. He turned the page and studied a map of the Fertile Crescent, soaking up every nuance.

Another turn of the page and William opened to the story of Genesis: the creation. A vivid illustration covered the title page; a lush green plain beside a clear, vast ocean, with birds and mammals and fish covering the Earth's surface. He began to read, reliving the first six days of Earth's creation; the light and the sky and the land and sea, the sun and moon and the animals and the humans, all fashioned in God's own image. On the seventh day, when all was well with the world, God rested.

William read as hours passed, remembering many of the stories from his childhood: Adam and Eve, Sodom and Gomorrah and the pillars of salt, the sacrifice of Isaac. There were familiar names like Abraham and Sarah, as well as people and stories that were completely new to him. He became immersed, lost in stories of ancient Egypt and the Promised Land, his own world disappearing about him. William only stopped reading when he felt a drop of water fall onto his current page.

He looked up at his ceiling, wondering if there was a crack, perhaps, and the rainwater was beginning to drip through. It took him a moment to realize that his eyes were swollen to the brim with tears and that a second one was about to break through.

"Holy shit," William thought. "Am I crying?" In the moment he gave himself to contemplate this question another tear fell onto the page. "Wow, I'm crying. Why am I crying?" But he knew.

It was nostalgia; a concoction not only of images and words that he had not seen since childhood, but the feeling of catching up on all he had missed. Stories of angels and miracles and prophets spoke to him, telling him that this was his faith and he had the power to bring it back into his life.

A teary-eyed William finished the story of David and Goliath and marked his page with a post-it note, shaking Damian's sleepy head off of his leg. His alarm clock flashed five forty-five, and William began to derive a plan of action, most of which was spontaneous. He wandered into the kitchen, turning up the radio and finding the biggest pot that he could, which he filled with water and put on the stove to boil. TV dinners were out of the question.

His dad came home around six-thirty, whistling quietly as he walked up the stairs to find William standing over the stove listening to *Market Place*, pasta boiling on one burner while a tangy tomato sauce simmered on another.

William drained the pasta into a fancy looking bowl and poured the sauce on top, leaving it on the counter to cool slightly while he took a loaf of French bread from the cabinet – the closest thing he could find to Challah bread – and cut it into thick slices. He rummaged through the cabinet above the sink to find his mom's china plates and set three places at the table, complete with fancy wine glasses and cloth napkins.

His dad looked pleased as he began to make his coffee.

"I'm doing Shabbat for Mom tonight," William announced proudly, as he placed a carton of grape juice on the table, filling each wine glass.

"It looks good," his dad told him, turning the coffee maker on and shuffling toward the living room. "You should do this every night."

William laughed a little as his father sank into the couch in the living room, his back to William and picked a book up off the coffee table. *War and Peace.* The front door opened again, about fifteen minutes later; the sound of the rain entered the house with William's mom.

"Hello!" she called, just as William was lighting the two tall candles that he had set in the middle of the table. "Did you make dinner?" She trudged up the stairs, stopping as she saw the table settings, her work bag tumbling to the floor.

"Yeah," William smiled. "Shabbat shalom."

There was a long pause. "Thank you, honey," his mom eventually said, giving him a hug that quite literally knocked the breath out of him.

"You're strangling me, mom," William said.

"Sorry. Let's eat."

William and his mom sat at the table, William's father lumbering over shortly after to take his seat. William and his mother recited the prayers over the candles and the bread and the honorary grape juice, their sing-songy voices drifting around the two small flames in the center of the table, intertwining with the smoke and rising to the ceiling.

"Shabbat shalom," Mrs. Spencer said.

# EIGHTEEN

Feelings from the previous night carried themselves to the Saturday morning sunrise and William awoke, contented and smiling, after a wholesome ten hours of sleep. His body was rested and his mind, normally judgmental or worrisome, was peaceful; for once not dreaming up reasons why the coming day would be disastrous. He stretched himself out, nudging Squeakers at the foot of his bed, and allowed himself to fall gracefully back into an unperturbed, dreamless sleep.

He woke again, a few hours later, to the distant hum of a lawnmower and a thin line of sunlight flowing gently into his room. He grunted, tossed around a few times and finally managed to push himself up, sliding out of bed and lumbering into the living room, giving himself a few seconds to adjust to the brightness.

It was a glorious suburban day, complete with chirping birds and screaming kids and the smell of cut grass wafting with the breeze, all made fresh by the previous day's rain. Every inch of the neighborhood that William could see was covered with a florid embellishment of lush trees or emerald grass or an abundant collection of dewy leaves. Everything was green.

William wasn't feeling particularly hungry and only desired to be out in the fresh air which beckoned him so unashamedly. He wandered back into his room to change into a white T-shirt and shorts, taking a moment to examine himself in the mirror. Though his modest conscience wouldn't allow William to say he was proud of his body, his mind would admit that he was. Years of athletics had treated him well, although he often wished for broad shoulders and more defined cheekbones.

Turning away from his curious reflection, William dug around the piles of mess that made up his room for his running shoes, which he found hiding under his bed. He slipped them on, feeling their familiar grip and comfort and wandered out of the house to the front lawn, neglecting his phone and his music and instead surrendering himself to nature. Sunlight blinded his sensitive eyes, though the fresh air was rejuvenating, quieting his busy soul.

He started jogging lightly down his street, shaking out his stiff legs as he passed one generic suburban house after another, their SUVs shining in the wake of their perfect gardens. Despite his weak, throbbing knees, William felt more awake and healthy–not just in a physical sense–with every step, breathing in the warm, growing spring scents.

He branched left off his street at the beginning of a bike path, following the paved trail downhill and through a short, dark tunnel that consistently smelled suspicious. For years, William was too afraid to enter the tunnel alone, scared off by the notion of bears or aliens or drug dealers in its depths, waiting to kidnap him or devour him alive. He realized, one day, that the tunnel was only about thirty feet in length and allowed a maximum of fifteen seconds to walk through. The chance of him being eaten by a bear was fairly minimal.

William reemerged into the sunlight unharmed, making his way between a towering wall of oak trees on either side of him, guarding his flanks as he dashed through the neighborhood, no particular direction in mind. He passed some people with dogs, a couple freshmen walking together, a man on a bike, his school, Emma's house. He waved to Jeremiah, who he saw behind the counter at Pitt's as he ran by.

After another two miles, the Hawthorne River scenery began to repeat itself and William stopped, breathing heavily. Despite the sweat and tufts of hair plastered to his forehead, William felt better than he had for a long time. He cut through the woods and made it to the bike path that stretched from the field behind his school to his backyard and beyond, casually walking through a few neighbor's yards until he reached his neighborhood's biggest street, Hawthorne River Road. He walked until he found a secluded house, its garden overgrown and its trees hanging over its roof protectively. Not thinking twice, he walked up the driveway and the front steps and knocked twice on Leila's door.

William glanced around quickly; there weren't any cars in the driveway, but Leila didn't drive yet. None of the lights were on, but that was normal. He ignored the fact that he was covered in sweat.

The door opened after a moment and Leila, in grey Georgetown sweatpants and a black tank top, blinked the sleep out of her eyes.

"Seriously, Will," she said, yawning. "It's the first day of spring break, and you're already awake and sweaty. How?"

William smiled. "I mean, it's sunny and springy and pleasant," he replied. "Why are you cooped up inside in your pajamas?" Leila shrugged, tugging her bangs out of the bun on top of her head. "Want to hang?" he asked.

"Let me put some real clothes on," she told him, leaning dazedly against the door. "I can meet you at school in ten minutes, I guess." William nodded, catching a few glances of the interior of her house. It was clean but standard, almost boring, with no art or music or NPR, very unlike his. Very unlike Leila.

"Yeah, cool," he responded, backing off the porch. "I'll see you then."

Leila smiled, closing the door slowly. "See you."

William walked, smiling, to his school, touching the leaves of the trees with his fingertips, feeling the dew seep down his skin. Though he often dreamed of something other than his small, suburban neighborhood, William appreciated days like these, when he was surrounded by nature and wholesome people. The quiet was especially good.

He reached the side parking lot of Hawthorne River High School, sitting in a vacant parking spot and gazing aimlessly into the sky as he tried to find a place where the great vacuum of space began. A butterfly landed on William's arm, staying for a moment to tickle his skin gently before dancing off into the breeze again, its paper-thin wings stronger than they looked.

William waited a few minutes before Leila walked up, her arms covered once again in a black long-sleeved shirt, her sweatpants exchanged for denim shorts. She squinted, as if she was still adjusting to the sunlight.

"Out of curiosity," Leila began, "why are we awake?" She stood with her arms crossed, scanning the empty parking lot. William rolled his eyes.

"Come on, it's almost eleven," he said. "How long were you planning on sleeping?"

"You'd rather not know." A vague smile crawled across her face. "So what are the moves?"

William shrugged. "Probably skydiving. BASE jumping. Ecstasy. Hardcore stuff."

Leila raised her eyebrows. "Yeah, I'm down for all of that. Except the ecstasy," she joked. "I've always wanted to go BASE jumping."

"Or we could just go for a walk?" William suggested, and Leila agreed.

"So why are you so energetic this morning?" she asked him as they left the parking lot of Hawthorne River and walked along the street, the sound of a nearby interstate highway rushing past them.

"Uh," William shrugged again. "I don't really know. I ran, so I feel good. It's spring break. Emma and I talked yesterday. I'm just more satisfied than I have been in months, and I'm not anxious or anything. It's pretty cool," he said with a sigh, realizing he had just given Leila a lot more insight into his life than he had intended. He saw that Leila was giving him a quizzical look and quickly added, "I'm not on drugs or anything."

She grunted, smiling. "I didn't think so."

William breathed another sigh.

"It just sounds like things were pretty rotten for you, even before the whole Cassie scandal." Her brown eyes searched his face through her bangs and William was caught off guard.

"Not even," he said, stepping on a crunchy looking fallen leaf. "I don't get it. My life is fine. I get good grades, I'm not messed up on drugs all the time. I'm not, like, bullied or anything. Maybe my dad can get a little too angry at times but I have nice parents who care about me and stuff. I should be leaping for joy every day but I only ever feel crappy and dismal and just freaking hopeless." He looked at Leila. "It's weird."

"It's hard for you to feel happy, isn't it?"

William nodded.

"You don't have fun at parties or anything? You sleep all the damn time." Again, William nodded, as Leila whacked each nail on the head. Then, "We're pretty similar, you and I."

William didn't say anything for a little while, just walked alongside Leila, his mind churning. A few cars zoomed past them, going at least fifteen miles over the speed limit. The neighborhood was otherwise quiet, aside from the thoughts screaming in William's head.

"Is something wrong with me?" he finally asked.

Leila giggled. "There's something wrong with everyone," she sighed to the sky. "Some people deal with it, some people let it deal with them." She turned her gaze to William's green eyes. "It might just be a teenager thing, you know. But, then again, the way you describe it makes it seem like something totally different. Maybe it's in your head."

William raised an eyebrow. "My head?"

"It's something about your brain producing too much of this hormone, or not enough of that one," Leila continued with a shrug. "Depression. It's weird shit."

"So you're saying I'm depressed?"

"I'm saying you should try to find out."

He scoffed. "How?"

Leila looked into his eyes. "You'll find a way."

# NINETEEN

"Favorite movie?"

William pondered for a moment, turning the question over in his head. "Uh," he pouted, concentrating. "Fight Club."

Leila nodded, her hands nimble as she braided her long hair to the side. "That's a good one, but we're not really supposed to talk about it," she said, sharing a grin with William. They each sat cross-legged on the dock that hung over Hawthorne River's hidden pond, bordered on all sides by tall reeds that whistled in the early spring breeze. Tiny fish hurried about the water beneath them, evading the box turtles that patrolled the area. A pair of geese hung by the dock, floating lazily on their feathered bellies, making ripples in the reflection of the trees that concealed the pond.

"How about…" Leila began, pausing to think and tie a small hair band around the bottom of her braid. "Favorite holiday?" She sat back, satisfied, pulling on strands of her bangs.

"Hanukkah," William answered immediately. He tossed a stone into the placid water, splitting the hydrogen bonds that held it together and smiled at the sight of Leila's apparent confusion. "What?"

"I didn't know you were Jewish," she admitted, puffing out her lower lip. William rolled his eyes, chucking another rock into the water.

"No one does," he said, honestly. "I mean, it's not very evident." Leila looked at him, quizzically, and he launched into the details.

"My mom's Jewish. So I am too, technically. But my dad isn't and he didn't really want to be involved in the whole religion thing. I used to go to Hebrew school and stuff, but I stopped, and after that we just stopped going to temple and celebrating the holidays and all." He shrugged.

"So you're a Hebrew school dropout?" Leila asked.

William mustered a smile. "I guess. It's my biggest regret."

"Did you have a Bar Mitzvah?"

William shook his head. "That's my second biggest regret." He placed both hands behind him and leaned his head back into the strength of the sun, eyes closed. "Maybe I'll get one later, when I'm really old," he said. One eye peeped open, and he saw Leila nodding.

"I've heard of people doing that," she told him. "It'd be pretty cool, I think."

They sat in silence for a moment, interrupted only by a shy turtle peeking its head above the pond's surface. It glanced around, beady eyes searching its surroundings before diving below again.

"What about you?" William asked, finally. "Favorite holiday, I mean."

Leila yawned, stretching her legs. "I don't know." She shrugged. "Thanksgiving. Because there's food."

"Right, food and family." William laughed, though Leila shook her head.

"I just like the food," she remarked, quietly.

William cocked his head, confused. "What, you don't like your family?"

Leila looked directly ahead of her, opening her mouth for a moment but deciding against speaking.

"What?"

She shook her head, exhaling. "No, I do." A moment passed in silence, and then another. The two geese that floated idly by the dock wandered their way onto the grass and a dragonfly buzzed in front of William's nose. Leila bit her bottom lip, her dark eyes unmoving. "I like my parents. I like my sister. It just doesn't feel real."

William, not even knowing that Leila had a sister, raised one eyebrow, utterly confused.

"I'm adopted," she said.

William suddenly felt that he and Leila were sitting atop a solitary mountain, their heads peering over the clouds and down the infinite descent to a ground that did not exist. Wind whipped their hair and danced away, singing a sad, lonesome melody. He felt the two of them were completely alone, only for a moment. He then proceeded to do what he did best, he said something stupid. "For real?"

"For real." Leila mustered what might have been a smile.

William's head was reeling with questions, though Leila seemed prepared and answered them before they could be asked.

"My parents weren't financially stable. They had been looking for jobs and living on welfare for a while, so when I was two, I think, they sent me to a foster home." Her voice was deadpan and unemotional, though she began to throw small stones into the pond, hurling them with increasingly excessive force.

"They wanted me to be able to have a future, is what they said." Leila winced as the impact from one of the stones caused water to splash up into her face. "Give me more opportunities and such."

William hugged his knees in to his chest. "Do you resent them?" he asked her.

Leila shook her head, a few strands of hair near her ears falling out of her braid. "I don't resent *them*. I resent the situation," she admitted and hurled her last rock across the pond. It arced gracefully, cutting through the air before it broke the water's surface and sank slowly to the bottom. "I resent the fact that they're still financially unstable, even after fourteen years." Tugging on the ends of her hair, Leila finally mumbled, "I mostly resent the fact that I don't even remember their names. Or their birthdays or where they grew up or anything. It seems wrong."

William was struck into silence, a pang and an abyss of guilt building in his chest, not knowing how she could stand to keep something of such magnitude to herself for so long. He felt a lump form in his throat and he was suddenly filled with pity that Leila would never want him to feel.

"I don't want to say I'm glad it happened," she said, biting her lip. "But... I guess I'm glad it happened. I like my foster parents. I like my sister. I like that I can go to a good school and go to college in a few years and have food on the table and nice clothes and stuff. I'm glad that I'm able to have a future now, and I'll admit that. But it isn't an easy thing to admit."

Leila laughed suddenly, wiping her cheeks with a sniffle. "Shit," she choked. "Am I crying?" She laughed again as another tear rolled unabated down her cheek. "Holy shit, I'm crying."

William froze up, not having the slightest idea of how to comfort a crying girl. "Uh," he started, searching his brain desperately. "Wanna get ice cream?" he finally suggested, figuring it was a valid proposition.

Leila laughed again and shook her head, causing more red strands to fall from her braid. "No, I'm good, seriously." She sniffed and wiped her cheeks with a sigh. "Tuh," she muttered, "You're the first person to catch me crying in years." She stifled another laugh.

William smiled along with her. "That must be as rare as seeing Bigfoot," he said. Leila stretched out on her back, resting her head on her hands.

"I'm not crying," she started. "Just releasing endorphins." She met William's eyes, and they shared a grin. "I'm not sad, though," she reassured him, her eyes following a robin that cruised overhead. "Just overwhelmed."

"Ah," William nodded. "I gotcha."

Leila's eyelids fluttered shut and she breathed in a deep sigh, relaxing her head on her hands. William stretched his legs out and leaned back, his arms behind him. He gazed lazily across the pond, his thoughts nullified by the gentle, tickling spring breeze and the a cappella croaking of a family of frogs. A few birds were conversing high above them and the only other sound to be heard were the tall reeds rustling together. It seemed like an acceptable quiet.

William stared down into the water, catching sight of a school of tiny fish darting below the surface. He noticed his own reflection: a vague outline of his slim shoulders and shaggy hair. He thought about the water, how it wasn't just blue or green but it was a painting of the scenery around it, reflecting all of the colors of the trees and the reeds and the sky.

His mind quickly stumbled back to Leila, pushing through the screen of humming cicadas and bird melodies. The more he learned about her, it seemed, the less he knew. Curiosity suddenly overwhelmed him.

"I'm going to ask you a series of questions that you may or may not be totally comfortable answering. In which case you may choose not to," he said, making up words as he went along. "They're going to be asked regardless."

Leila, still basking in the sun with her eyes closed, shrugged. "Proceed."

"What," William paused dramatically. "Is your favorite color?" he said with a sly grin.

"You're going to have to do better than that, Monty Python," Leila sniggered.

"Alright. Well I'm curious," William started again. "Was your sister adopted too?"

"No, she was born a year after I came here," Leila told him, squinting as she opened her eyes. "She's in seventh grade. Her name's Michelle. She's pretty rad."

"I didn't know people still used that word," William admitted.

"It's part of a dying language."

William shrugged, watching Leila pull herself back up and

dangle her legs over the edge of the dock, the bottoms of her shoes grazing the surface of the water. "Where were you born?"

"Boston."

"Boston? How'd you end up all the way down here, then?"

Leila smirked. "Storks."

William rolled his eyes, though with no actual malice intended. "At least you're a good sport," he admitted.

"Hey, I'll answer all your questions," Leila said. "Though my answers may not be entirely correct." They proceeded to glare at one another for a small amount of time, until William confessed, "I used to think that babies came from storks."

"Well, son, I think your life got a lot worse after you realized they didn't." She grinned at him.

"Stop distracting me, I had questions to ask," he snapped.

Leila put her hands up defensively. "Proceed."

"I forgot my question," William said, to which Leila smacked him across the head. "Ow, what the hell?" he exclaimed, turning to face her. Her face was frighteningly emotionless.

"Do you remember it now?" she asked him, not at all innocent.

William thought for a moment, his mouth spreading helplessly into a smile. The girl who had been crying earlier seemed like a fabrication of his mind.

"Yeah," he admitted, rubbing the back of his head. "And I *will* get revenge for this." Leila merely shrugged, seemingly impassive to the threat. "Tell me, madam," he began, folding his hands on his lap and suddenly making use of a British accent. "Did you have any other siblings before you were adopted?"

"No," Leila answered, her British accent slightly less pathetic than William's. "They figured I was a big enough mistake. They didn't need more, savvy?"

"I don't think they say that much anymore," William admitted, returning to his regular speaking voice. "I think it's just a little idiosyncrasy of *Pirates of the Caribbean*."

"It's just for emphasis," Leila said, honestly.

"Do you think about it a lot?" William asked, launching immediately into his next question. He scooted forward to the edge of the dock, crossing his legs while Leila began to braid her hair again.

"I've turned my life over in my head hundreds of thousands of times," she said, her fingers working nimbly around her bright red hair. "It's the first thing I think about when I wake up in the morning, if I even slept the night before. It keeps me up for hours." William watched her layer one piece of sunset over another. "I think it'll be the last thing I think about before I die, if I can remember it that long." She smiled at William. "That's just how it goes."

"Wow," he breathed, feeling inept and insignificant. "Honestly, when I wake up, I usually think about how shitty I feel." He scratched at the back of his head, wondering how mindless he sounded next to her. Leila laughed, keeping her mouth closed. "It's interesting to hear all of that from you."

She shrugged, securing the end of her braid with a hair band. "You might be the only one at school who knows," she said to him, nonchalant as if it wasn't her biggest secret.

William felt differently, though, like his significance had increased enough to be trusted. It wasn't like the friendship he had with Emma, where he knew everything about her life and her family because she simply didn't mind if he did. He felt like a noteworthy companion to Leila, not only because she had told him about her adoption, but because she felt he could handle it. It was the most delicate aspect of her life and she had just placed it in another set of hands that could easily smash it to bits. She had given it another chance to be broken, yet she didn't seem to regret it.

"I've deemed you trustworthy," Leila said, her dark eyes sinking into his skin.

"I'm glad."

They sat without talking for a while, both staring straight ahead, Leila's legs hanging lazily off the edge of the dock, William's curled up under him. Vivid scarlet strands of hair bustled around Leila's face in the breeze, dancing across her skin and hollow cheekbones. She blinked the sun out of her eyes while William tossed pieces of mulch and clumps of dirt into the pond, watching the ripples he created expand outward until they thinned to nothing. He was surrounded by rustling reeds and honeysuckles and the unique scent of Leila's skin. Her aura billowed toward him in the gentle summer gusts.

After a while, they helped one another up, and walked, satisfied, from the pond and the dock, up through the bike path that wove through the trees, going out of their way to step on crunchy-looking leaves and twigs. Leila walked on the right of William with her hands in her back pockets. The hair around her ears had fallen out of her braid again and now dangled down towards her shoulders, frolicking around to the rhythm of her steps.

William looked up at the canopy of trees, observing all the shades of green about him. The leaves were like Leila's hair, he thought, with all the different tones and colors and highlights. She seemed to stand out now, bright red against the green backdrop, glowing in the afternoon sun.

They emerged from the woods and the bike path, walking in comfortable silence across Hawthorne River Road and over to the front parking lot of their high school, inhabited only by a few cars and a lone skateboarder. Leila kicked a small rock down the road with her head tilted down, converse scuffing the asphalt stubbornly. She was elegant in everything she did.

"I'm glad you decided to sit next to me in art," she said, and William could tell she was.

# TWENTY

At around two-thirty the next morning, William turned off of Hawthorne River Road and onto his quiet little street, walking slowly under the wise, old trees. The waning moon hid behind a shadowy mass of clouds, its pallid light barely permeating through the dark conglomeration of shapes in the sky. Raindrops left over from the previous evening's storm dove gracefully from the leaves above William's head as he wandered back to his house, his hands in their rightful place in the pocket of his gray hoodie.

William felt differently; in fact, he hardly felt at all. The nervous thoughts that would have normally filled his mind on any other night were missing, a sensation that he wondered about, but only for a second. His mind was quiet; the voice in his head that normally hissed insults and slander was shut off and silenced and he moved forward slowly, without thinking.

William gradually became part of his surroundings, all of his energy sinking down below him into the paved asphalt. Roots grew beneath him, cracking the street and sinking into the ground below. He became a tree, watching over the neighborhood, seeing children leave their toy cars for real ones as they grew older, watching some of them sneak out to see their friends, and others sneak out to be alone. He left his body briefly, glimpsing the quiet street through the eyes of a wise old tree that had seen it all.

He dissolved into peace for a fleeting moment before feeling the ground under his feet again, feeling himself back in the body of his sixteen year-old self, walking normally.

William halted suddenly, panicking as he heard the rumble of a car engine starting at a house nearby. He was poised to jump out of sight, ready to find a hiding spot in a bush nearby, but he instead stood motionless as a deer in headlights. The headlights of his mother's Honda stared him in the face, blinding him. William was no longer at peace. He merely blinked, looking equally as appalled as his mom did, who gaped from the front seat.

"William?" she called, loud enough for him to hear but not quite loud enough to wake up any suspicious neighbors.

"Yeah?" he responded, trying desperately to push the guilt out of his voice.

"Get in."

William complied, avoiding his mother's glance as he sat down in the passenger's seat, taking extra precaution to shut the door silently. The engine of SUV rumbled through the silence that passed between William and his mom. The next few seconds that ensued were long and painful.

"I swear on my first-born child that I was not doing drugs," William said finally, wincing in preparation for a fierce interrogation. When he was met with silence, he tried, "Or drinking. I wasn't drinking. I wasn't even with anyone," he admitted, defeated.

"What were you doing, then?" his mom asked him. Her voice sounded tired and defeated, and the skin below her eyes was paper thin.

"Taking a walk," William said, honestly.

"At two-thirty in the morning?" She was obviously skeptical, but she seemed too tired and otherwise concerned to be angry.

"Yeah," he sighed, as she abruptly accelerated dangerously fast down the street, gripping the steering wheel with white knuckles. "Look, I swear that was all. I wasn't doing anything illegal or dangerous or whatever. I just..." William paused, biting his lower lip in frustration. "I couldn't sleep. So I went for a walk. Where are we going, anyway? Like, what's going on?" He waited impatiently for a response.

Finally, after turning onto Hawthorne River road and speeding down toward the nearest highway, William's mother responded quietly, "Emma's in the hospital."

William's stomach began to churn before he could even begin to process the words he had just heard. He tried to speak, but opening his mouth seemed suddenly dangerous.

"Neil called me a little while ago," his mother began, referring to Emma's dad. "She got hit by a car when she was out with one of her friends."

It seemed to William like all the air in the car had suddenly been sucked up through a giant alien vacuum. His brain froze, though his body began to shake violently. He buckled forward in his seat, clutching the back of his head with unsteady hands, unable to see or breathe evenly. Cannons fired in his stomach and a vicious wildfire began to spread through his spine, seizing control of his nerves. Panic rang in his ears like a gong.

He was spinning, falling into infinity with no sense of direction or any of the knowledge on Earth. His mind reeled, though his thoughts weren't clear enough to form questions. Only minutes before, he had been as peaceful as an old tree. Now, it felt like needles were digging into his skin, injecting him with terror.

"She's been at the hospital for a few hours, now," William's mother said, her calm voice a blaring juxtaposition next to her son's anxiety.

William paid little attention to her words, feeling that at any moment he might rip his own hair out. He couldn't open his mouth.

"She was unconscious when Neil called me, but the doctors said the injuries weren't horrible." She slowed down only slightly as the old Honda rumbled off an exit. "I was going to wake you up so you could come with me, but you weren't home."

William found enough energy to stay calm long enough to apologize. As his mother sped through a yellow light, he managed to ask, "What about Dad?"

His mother sighed, pulling into the local hospital's parking lot. "He was too tired."

William felt sick all over again, his mind shredding itself to pieces as he walked with his mother through the parking lot, silent in the sudden stillness of the night. This was not the midnight walk he had set out to take.

His breathing had calmed down slightly in the cool night air, but his heart rate escalated again as he walked through the sliding doors of the hospital, the fluorescent lights and waiting room chairs and the smell of rubbing alcohol overwhelming him. He followed him mother robotically. It seemed like his body had switched to auto-pilot when his mind lost all sense of function, and he could only listen helplessly as she asked to see Emma Phillips-Avery in room six.

William followed his mother and a friendly-looking nurse in faded scrubs across the emergency room in a dream-like fashion, hearing only muffled sounds as he trained his eyes on the floor. Holding his breath and remaining as calm as he could, William marched himself into room six, holding back a gasp.

Emma, who usually stood strong and commanding despite her small stature, looked tiny and fragile among the white sheets of the hospital bed. She was hooked up to all sorts of wires that, although he knew were helping her, looked like threatening monsters. Her skin was sallow and pale, and her darkened eyelids remained shut while a breathing mask covered her mouth and nose, cuing the small yet steady heaving of her chest. Her face and arms were bruised, the right wrist secured in a cast, and a series of crimson scratches covered her cheek and jaw line.

William lowered himself, shaking, into a plastic chair across the room, next to Randy who was fast asleep. His mother sat next to Emma's dad, Neil, who held a cup of coffee in one hand, wearing a stone cold expression. Emma's mother, Melissa, was asleep on his shoulder.

Overwhelmed, William leaned back against the wall behind

him, closing his eyes and taking a much needed deep breath. Hearing that his best friend had been hit by a car had been the most painful moment he could remember, until now. Seeing her broken, bruised body was another hurt entirely. It was an image that would remain in his head forever; whenever he would see Emma or talk to her or even think about his best friend, he would picture her lying in a white hospital bed, medical tubes of all kinds snaking around her tiny, fragile body, the cuts on her face sticking out sorely.

William stayed awake for another two hours, watching Emma breathe while his mother and Mr. Avery drifted to sleep, exhausted. He was only able to focus on the rising and falling of the sheets over Emma, making sure they didn't stop.

At a quarter after four, William became so plagued by the humming of the medical machines and the unsteady breathing of the tired family that he couldn't stand to be in the room anymore. He mustered the strength to push himself out of the chair and walked out silently, roaming up and down the empty halls of the hospital, his hands shoved into the big pocket of his gray hoodie, the only comfort he could find in the cold, formidable corridors.

William found his way to the waiting room and sat on a stained upholstered chair, wrapping himself up in gray fabric, his hood shadowing most of his face. He sat and breathed for a long time, otherwise unmoving, watching a few nurses shuffle around the tired, more or less vacant emergency room. Fatigue tugged on the back of his brain, but William couldn't bring himself to surrender to sleep.

He was too exhausted to be startled when a voice spoke to him out of the desolate, morning silence.

"Hi, Will," fellow junior Alex Manville greeted him, walking through the sliding doors of the emergency room, a coffee in one hand and a low-quality breakfast sandwich in the other. There were bags under his eyes, and William could tell that he had been up for quite a while as well. Alex sat down across from

Willliam, , his legs fidgeting nervously.

"Hey," William responded, slightly confused, though not willing to ask Alex why he was there.

"Did, uh, she wake up yet?" Alex kept his eyes focused on the floor, though William knew they felt the same stress and pain.

"No," he said, as gently as he could. They were silent, not daring to look at one another. "Were you with her?" he asked, not forgetting about the feelings that Emma had for Alex.

Alex nodded, his straight blond hair falling over his eyes.

"Just hanging out?" William inquired, curiously. What must have started as an exciting evening for Emma had so quickly turned into tragedy. It seemed even more unfair.

"Kind of," Alex replied, flashing William a modest smile for assurance. "We saw a movie."

William's spirits were lifted temporarily and a smile crossed his face, knowing that Emma would have been excited. He was curious and finally composed enough to formulate questions, but he felt like Alex wouldn't want to answer them, and neither of the boys had the heart to talk about the situation. Instead, William sat silently as Alex finished his sandwich, glancing back to Emma's room every so often.

The rest of the morning squeezed by slowly, like the sun was too tired to rise above the trees. Nurses began bustling around and a few patients fluttered in with broken bones and concussions, though none seemed to be in critical condition. William busied himself by reading a few of the tabloid magazines stacked next to him while Alex dozed off across from him, his shaggy hair shielding his eyes.

It was almost eight, and William was skimming through an article about upcoming summer blockbusters when his mother walked out of Emma's room, rubbing the sleep out of her eyes. William tossed the magazine aside, nudging Alex out of his sleep as his mom approached. She looked stressed and worn, but she managed a smile.

"I have to go get ready for work," she told them. "Mrs. Phillips went to get breakfast, and Mr. Avery's still asleep. You should go talk to Randy though; he looks like he could use the company." She squeezed William's shoulder sympathetically, giving Alex an affable wave. "Call me if anything happens."

William and Alex said goodbye and stood up begrudgingly, their tired bodies protesting as they walked across the waiting room to where Emma and her family were sleeping, waiting.

Randy sat alone at the far side of the room, breathing slowly and deeply, his eyes closed as he rested his head against the wall behind him. He looked up as Alex and William entered, giving them a feeble smile and gesturing to the bench beside him.

"Hey, dudes," he greeted, his ever-friendly voice scratched with fatigue and worry.

"Hey, Randy," William said gently, taking a seat beside Emma's brother. Alex sat on the floor next to William, his knees tucked up toward his chest. The sounds of the medical machines hooked up to Emma were overwhelming.

"Long night, huh?" Randy joked, though his face was worn and distressed.

"Definitely," William admitted, slumping back in his seat. "I can't even remember the last time I was actually asleep," he said, returning Randy's feeble yet warm grin.

They listened for a moment to the whirring of machines and the steady beeping that tracked Emma's heart rate. The hospital room, which had seemed like a looming monster just before now felt like a haven, they were tucked away safely in a place of healing where Emma slept, aided by the snaking tubes and wires. The whole night had seemed surreal, like a trance or a vivid dream.

"You really take shit for granted," Randy said, finally, gazing across the room at the small figure sleeping soundly on the hospital bed. "Not just life, but health. Normalcy. Stuff like that," he admitted. "It's sad that it sometimes takes a horrible accident to see what you really have."

"I know what you mean," William said, nodding in agreement.

"You know that things will still be the same," Randy continued, "but at the same time, everything is different, just because of what could have happened. And because of what you could have lost." He sighed deeply, closing his eyes as he rested his head against the wall behind him.

"Life is fragile," William said, and for once he believed himself. It was as delicate as the skin on Leila's arms, all scratched and torn and scarred. "People are strong though."

Randy smiled at William, and closed his eyes once more. William did the same, allowing himself to sink into a much needed sleep.

# TWENTY-ONE

"Hey, wench."

William peered through the fog in his vision and rubbed his eyes as he gave a mighty stretch, trying to wake his tired body up. It took him a moment to distinguish the beeping hospital machines and the ugly white walls; more specifically, the tiny, bruised frame of the girl that rested across the room. He looked up at the clock above the doorway, realizing that it was almost noon.

"Wench."

William sat up suddenly, searching around the room for the source of the scratchy voice that was speaking undoubtedly to him. Alex was on the floor beside him, sleeping soundly. Startled and dazed, William squeezed his eyes shut, trying to fully wake up his mind.

"Jeez, Will, I think you were knocked out longer than I was," Emma's voice said, finally reaching into William's brain and plucking him out of his trance. "That's pretty bad."

William looked over to where Emma was lying, the bruises on her face making cruel shadows when she smiled at him, weakly but genuinely. He sighed.

"Damn it, Emma," William said, covering his face in his hands as he stretched back against the wall. "I wait in the hospital with you for ten hours, and the first thing you do when I wake up is criticize me." Though he was tired and cranky, the sarcasm in his voice was discernible, as well as the relief.

"Don't be too offended, you're doing better than Alex," Emma said with a sly grin, doing her best to sit up in her bed. "How long have you been here?"

"Since two-thirty or three," William recalled.

"I think I missed your entrance, then."

William shook his head and said, with a friendly roll of his eyes, "How many times have I told you that you have to check yourself before you wreck yourself?"

Alex was beginning to stir, so William began nudging him awake.

"Ice Cube was the first one to tell me that," Emma said. "But I guess I'll give you credit, since you're the one I never listen to."

William laughed a little as Alex woke up slowly, looking around in a befuddled reverie.

"What freakin' time is it," he muttered to himself, taking a moment to realize that Emma was awake again. "Oh, shit. Hey."

William couldn't fade a wry smile as Alex and Emma bickered fondly for a moment, catching glimpses of their nervousness. He figured it wasn't his time to stay there, so he bid them both a farewell, promising to be back later with food.

"If you aren't back by eight tonight I'm calling the cops!" Emma attempted to holler after him.

The walk from the hospital was not a particularly long one, although he was fatigued from the long night.He said goodbye to Emma's parents and walked into the blinding sunshine.

William took his time and arrived home around a quarter to one, using the spare key hidden in the backyard to creep in through the door to be greeted enthusiastically by his dogs and by NPR blaring something about budget cuts on the radio. He let out a deep, much needed sigh and made his way to the couch, flopping down in front of the TV and turning on an episode of *How I Met Your Mother*.

William stayed in the same position for almost two hours, the idea of getting up and being productive too burdening to even think about. His mom came home around three and made William a sandwich, only to leave for work again at four. Before she could walk out the door, William called, "Emma woke up."

"How is she?" his mom asked as William finally managed to push himself off of the couch and into the kitchen.

"Sassy," he replied, taking a carton of yogurt, two apples and a few slices of cold pizza out of the fridge. He walked to the top of the steps with his arms full.

"I'll bring you over to visit a little later," William's mom said, opening the door. "I'll be home around six-thirty or so."

"Later, mom."

"Peace."

William subsided back to his spot on the couch for his after-lunch lunch, sticking around for another hour to watch an intriguing Norwegian mockumentary called *Trollhunter*.

William finally decided that being lazy was unsatisfying, and noticing that the food baby in his stomach was growing at a drastic rate, he rolled himself off the couch and slumped down the stairs, heading out the door once more and making his way toward Hawthorne River Road, ending up, indisputably, at the end of Leila's driveway. He walked up to the door and knocked, without a second thought.

A middle-aged man with a tired face and a bit of scruff lining his chin opened the door, looking slightly distressed, though his eyes were friendly. He was, William assumed, Leila's stepdad.

"Hi," he said.

"Uh, is Leila home?" William asked, scratching his head and trying to peer into the interior of Leila's house. He caught a glimpse of her younger sister, wide eyed and dark skinned, spying on him from the kitchen at the top of the steps.

"No, actually," the man at the door answered. "She should be home pretty soon, though. I can tell her you stopped by."

William nodded. "Yeah, sure, thanks. I'm, uh, Will Spencer," he said, without conviction. "Just so...if she asks...yeah."

The man at the door smiled. "I'll tell her you came over."

"Great, thanks," William said, and walked away feeling sufficiently embarrassed.

Not wanting to go home and rot in front of the television again, William headed over to Pitt's with a few dollars in his pockets.

The shop was fairly empty, only a few employees bustled about in the kitchen. Jeremiah sat behind the counter, his Pitt's Pizza visor pulled over his eyes as he gazed down at the screen of his iPhone.

"Mr. Spencer, my man!" Jeremiah called as William pushed through the door. "Look, the books are back!"

And indeed they were. The bookshelf that had taken a hiatus for a few weeks sat back in its usual corner, though it held quite a few bookless gaps.

"We know you're a book person, so we were hoping you could give us some suggestions on how to fill it up," Jeremiah continued. "You getting a bagel?"

William nodded. "And some Dew." He looked back at the bookshelf, contemplating the works of literature that could fill it up. "Can I make you a list?"

"Please," Jeremiah laughed, sliding a pen and a notepad across the counter to William. "Keep the sex, drugs and violence to a minimum, though. This is a family friendly environment."

William slid the money for the bagel and the soda across the counter in exchange and made his way to his favorite armchair beside the bookcase, grabbing a Mountain Dew from the nearby fridge and scribbling down the names of his favorite books feverishly.

*The Book Thief, Markus Zusak*
*The Hitchhiker's Guide to the Galaxy, Douglas Adams*
*Slaughterhouse-Five, Kurt Vonnegut*
*The Great Gatsby, F. Scott Fitzgerald*

By the time Jeremiah came by with the bagel, William had written at least fifteen titles, with even more on his mind.

"Keep 'em coming," Jeremiah said, taking a seat beside William, watching him scribble names onto paper for a while before speaking again. "You hear about Emma?" he sounded hesitant.

William stopped writing and sank back into his chair. "Yeah," he said, as if it were obvious. "How'd you find out?"

"I heard from Alex," Jeremiah admitted.

"Do a lot of people know?"

"At this point, probably."

William couldn't help picturing Emma lying unconscious, bruised and broken in an unfamiliar hospital bed, her faced crimson with scars and scratches. He shook it off, recalling her awakening that morning; her humor and good spirits, despite her injuries.

Jeremiah walked back to the counter when the phone began to ring so William looked through the bookshelf, pulled out an old *Calvin and Hobbes* comic book and got lost in childhood.

After an immeasurable amount of time, the door to Pitt's Pizza brushed open with a gust of fresh air, the scent of newly cut grass wafting in with the sound of a distant lawnmower as Leila stepped inside the small shop, a floral dress drifting delicately around her knees. She looked around for a moment. Small fiery streaks hung down from the messy-looking bun on the back of her head, the hair around her face making trails across her cheeks. Her shoulders were slightly sunburned, covered only by thin, blue straps. She looked more elegant dressed up, though no more beautiful than she did in her sweatpants.

It took her a moment to meet William's gaze, her dark eyes adjusting to the brightly lit interior as William put the book away and got up to meet her.

"Hey," he said, tossing his trash away.

"My dad told me you stopped by," she started, looking embarrassed. "I heard you usually come here. I don't stalk you though, I swear."

William managed a smile, though Leila's lack of expression told him that she was mildly serious. "I pretty much live here. Don't worry about it."

"I figured. They have food and books."

The two stood awkwardly in the middle of the store for a minute, the light of the muted TV on the wall screaming.

"We should go," Leila said.

# TWENTY-TWO

William leaned back against the wide trunk of the pine tree behind his house and inhaled deeply while Damian curled up in his lap. Leila lay across from him, resting on her elbows while she rubbed Squeakers' belly, gently humming what might have been a score from *Star Wars*. It was sometime around six, and it was beautifully peaceful.

From somewhere around the house, Will heard the engine of a car crescendo as it approached the front yard, leaves crunching beneath its wheels. It slowed to a gradual stop, rumbling impatiently.

"That should be Cindy," Leila said, picking herself up slowly. "Sorry I couldn't stay. Tell Emma to feel better."

"No problem," William said, standing up beside her with a yawn. "Thanks for, um," he paused, wordless. "Keeping me company," he added slowly, tentatively, wincing at his own words.

"Anytime," Leila nodded, making her way around the house while Will made his way to the back door. Leila waved once and hurried away, her elusive presence staining the images of William's mind.

Will's mom arrived a little bit later, stopping only to make a cup of tea before she and Will journeyed back to the hospital, bearing a Big Mac for Emma. They met Randy in the parking lot as he slugged over to Dan the Van.

"I've been appointed to Starbucks duty," he said with a feeble grin. "Emma will be glad for the food, though. She can be pretty ferocious when she's hungry."

Emma seemed calm enough, however, when she woke up from a nap as Will and his mom walked into her hospital room, acknowledging Alex off to the side.

"We brought you food," Will announced, taking the plastic

chair beside Alex.

"Aw, yes!" Emma exclaimed, trying her hardest to pull herself up to a sitting position. She winced momentarily in pain. "Thanks. No one else would get me anything. Only decaf Starbucks." She snatched the burger out of Will's hands.

"We just don't want you to throw up or anything," Alex said, pushing his hair out of his eyes.

"Now why would I do that?" Emma asked, taking a monstrous bite that annihilated a good quarter of the Big Mac.

Alex shrugged, resuming his slouched position.

"My belly is made of steel. It's like Superman. Supertummy," she said, shamelessly, finishing the burger up within the minute.

Emma's energy surged and Will and Alex were eventually permitted to push her around the hospital in a wheelchair, so long as they didn't crash into anything. To Emma's delight, this rule was broken instantly, resulting in a wild chase through the hallways. They wheeled her to the parking lot after escaping a few angry nurses, taking a moment to catch their breath and let out a few adrenaline-induced giggles.

"If we can find some other willing patient, I bet we could race," Emma mused, pushing a dark curl out of her face. "Doctors can place the bets." She laughed, breathless.

"You are so full of terrible ideas," William responded, dropping to the ground with a grin. "Some rules, oddly enough, are actually meant to be followed."

The delighted brunette shook her head, her eyes fluttering closed as she leaned back in her chair. "Nope," she breathed. "Nope, nope, nope."

They rested momentarily, energy flowing from their bodies into the ground below. No one spoke while the clouds passed gently over the sky, rolling softly with a passing breeze. William felt peaceful and satisfied, the warm air massaging his skin.

"So how's Leila?" Emma finally questioned, opening her eyes again.

Will raised an eyebrow, his lips forming a doubtful half-smile. "What about her?"

"How is she?" Emma asked again, looking at Alex with a coy grin. "Don't act like I don't know."

"Alright," William surrendered. "But how do you know?"

"She knows everything," Alex provided.

"I know everything," Emma supported, flicking William's cheek. "Best to skip the questions and just tell me."

William grinned, shaking his head at the ground. "Uh, she's well," he admitted at a loss for words. "She says feel better."

"D'aww," Emma cooed, "I knew you liked her."

"I didn't even say anything to imply that!" Will exclaimed while Alex and Emma snickered, sharing a look. "I never said I liked her."

"But you do," Alex tried to affirm.

"I don't know," William admitted to them as he admitted to himself. "There are a lot of things I don't know." He was brought back to the conversation he had with Leila about his mind and the hormones and the possibility of a silent, invisible disease that plagued him day in and day out. He had considered telling Emma, asking her about depression, but he figured that could wait.

Same," Emma sighed, biting her lip as she often did when in deep thought. "There's nothing wrong with that. At least, that's what everyone tells teenagers. 'You'll discover yourself when you get older!'" She said in a mocking voice.

"But we're always getting older," Alex chimed in, sitting next to Will. "So I guess we never really know anything for sure."

"Maybe," Emma shrugged. "Then again, maybe it just all plateaus when you reach a certain age. Like, when you turn fifty, everything just makes sense." She chuckled.

"Ehhh," Will laughed, "I don't think it works like that." He was silent for a brief moment while Emma and Alex waited patiently for him to continue. "I don't think knowledge is definitive, that's all. Especially not knowledge about yourself," he went on timidly. "We don't even know *what* we know, if that makes any sense. And it's not all supposed to be discovered, I guess. There will be things we never find out, and there are things that we already have. We can't be expected to know everything, but we should at least make a conscious effort. If I don't know who I am, then no one else does."

Stillness ensued, a state of being not only characterized by lack of movement but also by silence and conscious reflection. While William's words soaked into Emma and Alex's mind, Will himself was still fighting to understand what he had said. The words hadn't been prompted or thought out, they were simply stated when William opened his mouth.

"That was like, philosophical type shit, dude," Alex said.

"Good company brings out the philosophers in us," Emma chimed in with a sly grin. "Speaking of which, do you ever think about clouds?" she asked, with her eyes turned skyward.

"Uh," Alex gave her a quizzical stare. "I don't...not really...what?"

"They're just so nice. Like little floating sheep."

"*Big* floating sheep," William added. Looking at Alex, he whispered, "I think it's the pain meds."

They watched a few cars pass, watched the sun sink elegantly down behind the towering hospital building. A tender breeze combed through William's hair as he drifted into a thoughtless state of mind. He let his senses open, let the warm evening air climb gently over his skin, massaging him further into a state of calm. His breath was full and even. His mind was quiet, not flooding with thoughts and worries. He watched the sky change color.

"Look, Randall's back," Emma said, suddenly, snapping Will out of his peace of mind. "What took him so long?"

Randy hopped out of his van, making his way across the parking lot in his typical meandering way, carrying a few drinks.

"Sorry I'm late," he called, walking toward Emma, Will and Alex. "Dan had a moment in the middle of the highway. They had to call the cops and everything. It was a big clusterfuck." He handed out Starbucks cups.

"What, did he stall?" Emma asked.

"Yep."

"Vans," she shook her head, taking a long sip. "We should probably go back inside, anyway. We told the nurse we'd just be a few minutes." She laughed.

They walked back in together, with Alex wheeling Emma at a legal pace. The waiting room was busy again, stocked with crying children and their disgruntled parents. A few teenagers hacked away at their smartphones, despite broken limbs. Mr. Avery walked out to meet them.

"Where've you been, Randy?" he asked, stealing a sip of Will's coffee.

"Big jumble on the highway with Dan," Randy responded, which seemed to be a sufficient answer.

"Well, we were just talking to the doctors. You got one more night here," Mr. Avery said to Emma. She groaned, unenthusiastically.

"Maybe we'll just move in here," Randy teased, receiving a threatening glare. "Since you seem to love it so much." Emma didn't need words to reply.

"It's just one night," Will tried. "They'll even feed you." Emma simply grumbled.

William's mom approached from across the waiting room, keys in hand, gently squeezing Emma's healthy shoulder.

"You'll be out soon," she reassured her. "I think William had better be going though. Feel better, sweetie."

She and Will thanked everyone for putting up with them, wishing the Phillips-Avery family the best. Emma even spared a smile, though there were obvious undertones of disappointment behind it.

The two walked back to the car silently, driving home in a gentle, weary state. Will's mom, after pulling up to the house, stopped the car but remained as she was, looking at the dashboard in silence. Will remained seated, curious.

"Can I ask again why you were outside the other night?" William's mother asked, biting her lip in painstaking anxiety. William raised an eyebrow, paused, understood.

"What?" he asked just for the sake of it, making it clear his confusion wasn't genuine.

"The other night, before we went to the hospital," she explained, trying to maintain her composure. "You were walking up the street. It was like, two a.m."

"Oh," William admitted shakily, racing through his memories for a valid excuse. Finding none, he began candidly, "I wasn't smoking anything." He began to tense up instinctively, feeling the color saturation in his cheeks grow deeper.

His mom nodded, turning back to the dashboard of the car. "That's a good start." She continued to wait in silence, the kind that slammed an iron fist upon a table, demanding answers. Will fidgeted desperately, surprised as the truth began to pour hesitantly, inevitably from his lips.

"I was, uh," he cleared his throat, seeing every memory of his midnight walks scroll across the inside of his mind. "Taking a walk."

"You were taking a walk in the middle of the night," his mom replied, stating what should have been a question.

"Yeah."

The silence roared like a mad crowd.

"Any specific reason?" Will's mom asked, raising her eyebrows in suspicion. Her eyes continued to stare straight ahead.

"No. No, not really."

"So you just take walks at two in the morning, then?" his mother asked, struggling to maintain her initial sternness. "What, for exercise? Fresh air?" She directed her gaze to William for a moment, her stare unwavering.

"I do, actually," William admitted, quietly, feeling the satisfaction of letting go of a secret that silently crept through his mind day after day. "It's kind of a hobby."

His mom opened and closed her mouth several times before finding words. "I don't...what?"

"Because no one talks to me then," Will stated firmly, slamming down a metaphorical fist. "It's great. And no one expects anything of me, and I don't have to act a certain way. There's no sitting around and watching my friends get high." His voice was beginning to grow exponentially, the pre-programmed excuses dissipating against the truth. "There's no one to impress and no standards to conform to. It's just me, doing whatever suits me, not being subservient to some social code that says I have to be a man and not a boy. It's the only time that doesn't actually suck, because there's no one around to ruin it. This town is a fucking mess, and that is the only way to avoid it." He took a deep breath, feeling the sensation of letting go.

William's mom remained speechless, chewing her thoughts over and over in her head. She turned to her son, opened her mouth, closed it, turned away again. Her breath was loud and stressed.

William shrank back into the seat of the car, almost grimacing, wishing he could suck the words back in. Instead, they floated around him, invisible and irrevocable. The silence seemed to stretch for hours.

"Are you lonely?" his mom asked finally, the muscles in her face finally relaxing. William raised an eyebrow in suspicion, though the words struck him hard.

"No. Why..." he began immediately, trailing off as he let a commanding honesty take hold of his conscience. "Sometimes."

His mother inhaled deeply. "Are you sad?"

"Sometimes."

"More often than not?"

William paused. He contemplated lying, but the idea didn't settle. Honesty was irreversible. "Yeah."

The sound of his mother's anxious breathing pounded in his ears. He saw her mind turn upside down, her reality reverse.

"I always thought you seemed really happy," she admitted to him, after a careful consideration of her words.

"You also thought I spent my nights sleeping," William muttered.

"Well, is anything bothering you?"

"Um, not particularly." Will reached for the door handle, but his mom shot her hand up, finally turning her eyes to her son. She waited another moment to sift through her thoughts.

"You know," she began, taking in another deep breath. "I was pretty depressed when I was a teenager." Her words came out slow and stuck together.

"So?" Will shrugged, casting his eyes downward. "Aren't most people my age?" Skepticism seeped from his voice.

"Well, they might feel depressed sometimes. But it's a real illness, and it can be genetic." William didn't speak.

"So I'm worried."

"Cool," Will answered, obviously distressed. "Cool. Thanks, mom." He leaned over and opened the door, stepping outside where the cool air invited him.

"Wait," he heard from the car.

"What?"

"Will you talk with me tonight?" Despite her unceasing inquiry, she seemed genuine.

"Yeah, sure," William finally agreed, Slamming the car door behind him. His mother's words, along with those of Leila, were beginning to consume him.

# TWENTY-THREE

An empty cereal bowl and a lagging Xbox accounted for the rest of William's evening. Sprawled across an old pull-out couch, William buried himself in his basement, lounging in his sweatpants while Kurt Cobain flooded out of his laptop. His hands hacked away aggressively, weary eyes never straying from the screen ahead of him while he struggled to keep his parents' arguing voices upstairs from seeping into his head. Though he wasn't particularly invested in *Call of Duty*, William felt he needed an excuse to shoot something.

Heavy footsteps began to make their way to the basement, and William looked up to find his father standing in front of him, looming tall as he always did.

"It's for you," his father said, handing William a cordless telephone. William sighed, muted his laptop and answered.

"Hello?" his voice scratched.

"Hi, Will." The man on the other line was recognizable, but William was not quick enough to put the name to the face. "It's Mr. Monroe."

William panicked briefly, instinctively clearing his throat and flattening his hair down, though it was evident that appearances could not be seen through the telephone. "Hi," he answered slowly, with considerable caution. "Did I—"

"You're not in trouble," Mr. Monroe answered quickly, with what William could assume was an accompanying smile. "I wanted to talk to you for a moment. I just found something of yours recently and I mean to ask you about it."

William panicked again, leaping from the couch to pace nervously around the room, dodging a frantic Damian and one of his toys.

"Uh," he hesitated, trying to speak in his normal voice. "What, uh, what is it?"

"Well," Mr. Monroe began, evidently shuffling through some papers. "It looks like a story."

William remained stone cold and motionless. The color drained from his grimacing face. "What story?"

"Um, it looks like you were writing it." There was a painfully awkward silence, wherein William bit his bottom lip violently. He cursed himself in silence as the feeling dripped from his body. "The dead uncle," Mr. Monroe prompted him. It was called 'Chapter Three.'"

"Oh, right," William replied, wanting to smash the phone on the ground and catch the next bus to Baltimore and never be seen again. Instead, he shut his eyes tightly. "Yeah, that...that was mine."

"Well, I read it," Mr. Monroe admitted, a tinge of embarrassment traced his voice. "I apologize for not respecting your privacy but it was really..." he paused. "Really profound. Honestly. I was impressed."

"Oh." William loosened his fist, which he realized he had been clenching violently. "Thanks."

"I mean, I just saw it lying around and I physically cannot resist reading things and I was just astonished. I kid you not." Mr. Monroe paused, and it finally occurred to William how odd it was to talk to one of his teachers on the phone. For the longest time, he hadn't even considered the idea that teachers had lives outside of school. "It was great. Just great. Is there more?"

William laughed, feeling a considerable, tangible weight fly from his shoulders. "Uh, yeah," he said, with a growing smile. "Yeah. This is really embarrassing."

"Sorry," Mr. Monroe apologized again. "You've been doing great work all year but this," he sighed, obviously incredibly content. "This was totally unexpected. But really great. You're a very talented writer."

"Thank you," William said, meaning it.

"You could bring me whatever else you've written," Mr.

Monroe told him, his voice unexpectedly comforting. "I'd be happy to edit it. Or just read it." He laughed. "I like reading things."

"I figured."

They hung up and William flung himself back onto the couch, embarrassed beyond belief but ever so slightly proud, and still baffled by the fact that he'd just had a conversation with Mr. Monroe over the phone.

Realizing he had been holding his breath, William slowly exhaled all of the tension from his body, suddenly discovering a new appreciation for his English teacher. He was mortified but grateful, mostly relieved that his work had not been discovered by anyone else. He tried to imagine Kris reading it.

The heat in William's face gradually began to fade and he regained enough control of his hands to unpause his game, feeling much more at ease when he was able to blow the heads off a few zombies. He didn't allow himself to think any longer.

Much later, William could hear light footfalls descending the staircase. His mom appeared in the doorway, standing expectantly before William in an ancient pair of red flannel pajama pants that were fraying rapidly. Her normally strong, straight back seemed to hunch under some invisible burdensome weight. She smiled at William.

"Who was that?" she asked, referring to what William assumed was the phone call.

"Oh," William paused his game again, slouching back against the cushions. With great moral compromise, he resisted the urge to lie. "Mr. Monroe, my English teacher."

His mother crossed her arms, looking puzzled. "What was he calling about?"

"Um, he just read something of mine and wanted to tell me I did well." This wasn't entirely untrue, but it could be subject to easy misinterpretation.

"He just called to compliment your work?" his mom asked.

William nodded obediently, praying she would leave it at that. "Well, that was nice of him."

William let out an audible exhale. His fingers continued to punch the controller, though with significantly less force. "Yep." He kept his eyes locked on the screen.

His mom sat on the upholstered chair beside him, her small frame sinking quickly into the plush green fabric. She watched him play, remaining silent as her son slaughtered ruthless hoards of dead things. Once or twice, she took her phone out to check the time, waiting patiently for an opportune moment to interject.

"Soo." William began to fidget out of habit. Her silent observation was freaking him out; similar to the way a teacher would when standing over William's shoulder, looking at his work. "What's up?"

His mom smiled through her perpetually tired eyes. "Nothing," she sighed. "What are you playing?"

"What were you and dad bitching about?" William retaliated, instinctively.

"Don't curse, William," his mom snapped, suddenly defensive. "You don't have to act like it's a big deal. Married couples fight."

"Married couples fight every day?" William asked, oozing with skepticism. "How about happily married couples?"

His mom scowled, her mouth forming a thin, tense line. William could tell she was chewing over a retort in her head, but she decided to let it out silently with a deep exhale. "Does it bother you?" she asked.

William's hands began to shake again. He stared directly ahead so as to evade his mother's glance, wanting terribly to say yes. "No," he lied.

"When you're married, you have to live graciously with the things that aren't perfect," she explained slowly.

"I don't even know how to live graciously and I'm not married," William remarked distantly, passionately firing a barrage of bullets into the throat of an approaching zombie. "I'm not a psychopath, right?" he asked, searching gingerly for confirmation.

"No," his mother responded. "Just a high-functioning sociopath."

William smiled at the reference. "Thanks, Sherlock." He took a break from thinking and instead spent a moment focusing solely on shooting animated antagonists. "But actually," he continued cautiously, carefully choosing his words like he was sidestepping hot coals. "Does it bother *you*?" He turned to his mother as his character collapsed in a pixelated pool of blood.

William's mother stared straight through him with her characteristically tired eyes. "We're working on it," she admitted tentatively. "There have been some rough spots, but nothing unfixable. You don't have to worry."

William snorted. "I don't have to worry," he repeated with quiet contempt. "I wish I could convince myself of that."

"What's that supposed to mean?"

He shook his head, putting his controller down and rubbing his eyes. "I can't even think of the last time I wasn't worried. About anything," he added. "Literally anything that could possibly be worried about, I worry about. Even the small, petty things seem to drive me over the freaking edge. I literally..." William's words ran dry. "I can't function. Every minute my mind is just going, going, going, panicking about something that doesn't even matter, that I *know* doesn't matter yet I can't seem to stop myself from freaking out about it." He sighed. "It's exhausting."

William's mother waited patiently to reply, nodding her head slowly. "How come this is the first time you're telling me this?" she asked, more out of concern than offense.

"I—" William stopped, finding it useless to lie any more. "I just thought there was something wrong with me."

His mother stared straight through him again. "Tell me more."

# TWENTY-FOUR

*"My mind is a plague,"* William scratched into an old notebook. *"My thoughts are the victims and my actions reciprocate the damage. My mind isn't right. I'm not sane. I am undoubtedly lost."* William was silent, looking up from the lined paper in front of him. Sitting cross-legged on his bed, he stared out his window to the street, brushed with night, where the cool air and empty solitude beckoned. William placed the notebook under his pillow and got up, moving in an almost ghostlike manner out of his room and into the hallway. This time, however, he made his way to the back door, stepping out onto the stone patio.

A light mist grazed William's skin with an invigorating sensation and crickets made music around him. In the woods ahead, the trees whispered to one another in an ancient, sacred language. In his mind, William gathered his resentments: his anxiety, his cowardice, his lack of social competence, his sadness, his reality. He resented his growing impatience with the small town that he no longer fit into, the fact that he had all but lost his religion. He resented the fact that no one really knew him entirely; not Emma, not Leila, not even his own mother. William resented the fact that he was only happy when he was lost in his books, submerged in worlds and stories that he could not physically reach.

*"I was born on the wrong planet,"* he thought. *"I was never meant to wait around in school for twelve years and then sit at a desk for the rest of my life. I'm not equipped to change this world."* He thought back to his childhood, when it was believed that one could achieve anything if they worked hard enough for it. "Anything is possible," he was told. "No matter who you are or where you come from." An underprivileged, uneducated child could grow up believing he could study medicine at Georgetown and find a cure for cancer.

Uncovering this lie was a bitter manifestation of what would really be.

William leaned back against the sliding glass door, heavy eyelids falling shut over his skyward-tilted face. He remembered wishing that he would one day step outside and hear music rising in the distance; a flashing light would accompany a sudden gust of wind and he would be whisked off, suddenly and inexplicably, to another world. He would land in the pages of one of his books and stay there forever, riding horses or swinging swords around in good company, feeling entirely fulfilled. He imagined waking up elsewhere one day, some place limitless.

William opened his eyes again, greeted by the dim outlines of the chairs on his back porch and his mother's garden and farther back, a wall of trees. There were no mountain peaks in the distance; no rolling hills or hastening river etching itself into the ground. There was no big city, just a quiet, sheltered suburban wasteland.

William lifted his eyes to the sky above him, where grey clouds merged with velvet night, only a few speckled stars shining weakly through the dark veil. A breeze chilled his skin, brushing his unkempt hair aside. He stared past the crooked tree tops and beyond the clouds, looking farther into the sky than he had fathomed before. The color came in layers, with blackness giving way to lighter blues and rusted violet and eventually the piercing silver of a half-moon, which captivated William's vision.

He looked deeper, thoughtless but with intent, until he saw the very edges of the sky meet in the center, curving downward gracefully in a massive dome. The vastness of the universe exposed itself, and William felt his entire body shiver, feeling at once very small.

To his surprise, he wasn't daunted, he wasn't intimidated, and he all at once wasn't without hope, for his mind traveled back suddenly to his favorite books; of Frodo, whose character had fascinated him since childhood. That you could make such a powerful difference despite your size, whether literally or metaphorically, was an idea that sparked a sudden, and very powerful, force in William.

The night sky was all it took.

William no longer felt the wind; he felt nature's breath upon his face, bestowing in him a new self. He wasn't a weight upon the ground, he was a person, and all people had purpose. He looked up once more to the domed sky and the edge of the universe and smiled; maybe at God, maybe at the stars, perhaps at the sheer beauty and mystery of the nighttime.

He began to feel conscious of all of his previous misunderstandings; while his mis-wired mind aimed to guide him in the wrong direction, it did not control him. His supposed depression and worries weren't attached to him with the stigma of his person. He was William, not somebody with a messed-up brain. Not somebody who was mentally ill, but a soul who could mentally recover.

"Thank you," he whispered quietly, thought he did not know exactly to whom. Confused as he was, for as far as he was concerned, nothing had actually changed, more hope and purpose flowed through William than he had ever experienced. There had always been something about the night\that compelled him and confounded him, but it took perspective and a little proportion to fully understand its power.

A smile grew across his lips and William filled up with an unexplained happiness that expelled all the gloom from his body. Whether he was on the wrong planet or not, he felt a sudden sense of belonging. While he may have yearned for a new place outside of his sleepy Maryland town, he was glad for his childhood in Hawthorne River; the seemingly endless summer nights of dancing fireflies and the stillness of the woods after a snowfall had nurtured him, even after thoughts of big cities and shining lights began to grow in his mind. Here was home.

"Thank you," William whispered one more time to the sky, stepping back inside and closing the door. He felt entirely different: lighter and kinder with a new energy that stirred his soul. He couldn't exactly identify what had changed; after all, all it had taken was a porch and a night sky. He felt a new respect for the life that had been given to him, and William suddenly felt happy again.

# TWENTY-FIVE

William knocked on Leila's door for the second time the next day, having a little trouble maintaining his countenance as he made a rather unsuccessful attempt to smooth his hair down. He had stopped by earlier around eleven, after a bagel at Pitt's with Emma, to be greeted by Leila's stepfather, who kindly informed William that Leila wouldn't be home until later that afternoon. William spent the next few hours walking his dogs and going for a short run himself, later finding a mossy spot by a gently flowing creek to write.

Grounding himself atop a few large rocks, William isolated his creative ideas, pushing all else aside as he focused on scribbled cursive, his heart beating in sync with the flowing water and steady pulse of a woodpecker's percussion. In two hours another chapter and the beginnings of the next had been conceived. Quietly, the scratching of his pen harmonized with nature.

*"It'll only be a couple weeks," Ross said, the remorse in his voice trying urgently to compensate for the audacity of his actions.*

*Edwin couldn't find much to do besides shake his head, disbelief beginning to flow into his brain. "A couple weeks is nothing to you," he stabbed. "Time is nothing to you, you can't possibly..." he stopped, sputtering, trying to morph thoughts into coherent sentences. "Being here is bad enough," Edwin spat out, clutching chunks of his dark hair in frustration. "Being here alone? Yeah, no, you can't do that. I can't do that." He sat himself down beneath the tall oak that he had broken his hand on months earlier. His breathing was sporadic and short.*

*"Christ, Ed," Ross responded, slouching heavily with his hands wedged into his pockets. "A couple weeks is eternity to me. I'm not trying to make you miserable, there are just some things I have to do. They just can't be compromised."*

"This whole death business doesn't make any sense," Edwin found himself saying. "I thought you were a blessing, but this whole thing is evolving into a giant clusterfuck. I just..." he stalled, his hands clutching his head desperately. "I can't. I can't be by myself."

"But you're not," Ross told him. There was an intriguing silence. "You never have been. And you aren't ever going to be."

"That...no." Edwin shook his head. "That doesn't make sense. You're leaving. You left once and you're leaving again."

"And I returned, didn't I?" Silence. "You can't feel it now, but you will. I'm there, always."

William returned to reality when the door swung open suddenly, and Leila stepped out, leaving the sound of a petulant little sister behind her.

"Hi," she greeted him rather bashfully, concealed beneath an oversized sweater. Her face was flushed more than usual, her lips pressed tightly together.

"Hi," William replied. "You doing anything?"

"Not now," she admitted, and William could see that she looked as if she had no desire to leave her house. She was simply too polite to say otherwise.

"Wanna walk?"

"Sure."

They headed along the road toward the highway this time, wandering instead of explicitly going. All around them, suburbia was thriving; scents of cut grass and honeysuckle accompanied the gentle air. The atmospheric freshness was profoundly invigorating.

They walked in silence for a time; Leila carefully watching her steps beside William, who gazed into the pale-faced sky. They wandered out of Hawthorne River, crossing a lonely highway and travelling farther on. They passed idle parking lots and small office complexes that seemed to have been unused for years.

The two arrived eventually at an open grassy area, where

they climbed to the top of a hill and sat, finally, overlooking what seemed like the whole town. It was quaint, peacefully, but William knew it was not quite enough.

"What was the happiest moment you've ever experienced?" he questioned suddenly, letting his head rest in the grass as he lay onto his back.

Leila chewed this over. "I don't think I've had one yet."

William shrugged at her acceptable answer. "I thought for a while that I wouldn't have one. Like, ever." He took a deep, fresh breath. "It was the kind of thing where I was like, damn, why wasn't I born in Middle-earth or something, you know? This shit is lame." He heard Leila chuckle. "And I'm being totally serious. I thought that the only good stuff happened in books and that I would never quite reach an acceptable level of fulfillment, or whatever. But I don't think it's that way. Stuff only happens when you're there to let it happen to you." He was slightly embarrassed and a little bit proud of this statement.

"Deep," Leila said, letting the lone word float off into space.

"Think about it."

Leila appeared to be thinking about it.

"What are you getting at?" she inquired. "Did you just have the happiest moment of your life?"

"Not really." He shrugged, closing his eyes. "I think I'm just seeing things differently."

William tried to come up with a way of telling Leila. Finding no eloquent solutions, he finally admitted, "'Cause I decided to stand on my porch last night."

Leila giggled a little. "What? How…I'm missing something," she said. "Elaborate."

"There isn't much more to say," William admitted. "I went outside at night and stood on my porch and I looked up at the sky and I just felt different," he said. "It's like I saw the entire universe and how big it was and I realized I can *do* stuff. Like, there's so much I can do and I didn't even know it."

"And you just kinda figured that?" Leila questioned, obviously skeptical.

"I don't know what happened. Maybe it was some kind of divine intervention," Will said excitedly. "But something told me to quit bitching about insignificance because there is just so much stuff I can do." He turned to look at her, smiling. "Literally so much stuff."

"Were you tripping acid then?"

"Nope."

"Are you tripping acid now?"

"Nope."

"Wow!" Leila nodded.

William was aware of how ridiculous he sounded and he could see the indifference in Leila's face, but he could feel the gears in her mind grinding, contemplating the idea that William might actually be right. He closed his mouth, allowing ample time for the idea to soak completely into Leila's mind.

"Here, look up," he said, pointing straight above him to the dome in the sky. "See how the sky seems to meet at one point directly above you? It like, curves in and makes this dome shape."

Leila raised an eyebrow but looked above her, straining her eyes. "The hell?"

"Look harder."

She did, and William felt immense satisfaction as she began to nod, pointing up above her the way William was. "Holy shit, I see it." She laughed. "Whoa, that's cool. I never noticed."

"It's always centered right over the person who's looking at it," William observed. "Doesn't that make you feel special?"

"In a way, I guess so." She shrugged. "I can't stop looking at it."

"Sometimes, that's all you need," William said, leaning back and closing his eyes. "We're not insignificant, you know."

"Why, because we have our own little domes?"

William shrugged. "Those domes are pretty big."

"I'm pretty small."

"So was Frodo," William said, almost out of instinct. Leila turned her head, gave him a funny look and laughed.

"That makes me feel better," she replied, pulling her hair out of its loose, low ponytail and letting it fall below her shoulders. She started humming quietly to herself and William breathed in the pure tones, relishing every note. Her soft melody hung around them for a while, gradually drifting off with a sinuous breeze. Quietly, she began to sing, tender words strung together by a beautiful voice flowing from her lips.

William couldn't quite make out all of the words, but he felt every emotion that had been stitched into her song.

"You're a good singer," he told her.

She stopped, sighing. "You're a good person."

"I'm alright."

* * *

It was early evening when William and Leila found their way back to Hawthorne River Road. They had spent the rest of the afternoon exploring the woods nearby, climbing trees and releasing a long-lost childhood that had been hiding within them. Leila began to sing again as they walked down the street, passing the familiar sights and sounds that for once felt like home to William, no matter how much he yearned for more. He had been nurtured by this small Maryland town, and in time he knew he would learn to fully appreciate it.

William walked Leila to her house, giving her a final smile before he turned to leave.

"I'll do it tonight," Leila called to him, one hand on the door handle. William raised an eyebrow, confused. "The porch thing. The dome. I'll try it."

William felt himself grinning. "Do it," he said. "Just see what happens. You might be surprised."

"I'm sure I will be," she told him, genuine. "I'll see you later."

"Bye, Leila."

William turned for home, walking down the sidewalk along the line of trees that watched over him protectively, hearing and seeing all and yet not telling. He held his hand out, feeling the leaves, smooth between his fingers. Grass was growing through the cracks in the pavement, erupting out of the concrete shell.

William thought of himself as the grass then, and the trees that listened and even the air that gave life to all things. He didn't even need to leave his town to see the remarkable; it grew all around him.

When he walked in his front door, he was greeted by only his mother.

"Your dad went out," she responded, before William could even ask. "How was your day?"

William didn't bother to inquire any more. "Good," he said, a break from his usual "fine."

"Do you have plans tonight?" his mom asked, reclining on the living room couch with a bag of whole wheat pretzels.

"Nope."

"Wanna go to synagogue?"

William was almost taken aback. "Where?"

"I figured it's just us and we haven't been in a while and maybe you wanted to go. I found that children's bible in your room. Have you been reading it?"

William smiled. "Yeah. Yeah, we should go. I won't know what's going on, but I'll give it a shot." He laughed. "It's been a while."

"Well, no one said we can't try again," his mom said. "It's Shabbat, anyway."

William had almost forgotten what day it was.

"Might as well give it a go."

William was elated. "Let's go."

# TWENTY-SIX

When school started up again, William walked through the front doors that first morning in his typical fashion; tired, of course, with an overwhelming desire to be back in bed. He was irked a little by the shouts and unnecessary exclamations he heard around him and he was a little embarrassed by his sloppy appearance, but for once, his entrance was not accompanied by a looming feeling of dread.

He made his way to Mr. Monroe's classroom, weaving in and out of crowds of people, even catching a few greetings here and there. Mr. Schwartz hobbled past him cheerfully, calling, "Good morning, Mr. Spencer! Do you have your articles?"

William smiled. "I do." He spied Emma and a few friends chatting quietly in a corner.

"Hey, prostitute!" she called.

"Morning, whore," William replied casually, noticing that he and Emma were on the receiving end of some weird looks. He promptly walked to class, shrugging off a grin.

Mr. Monroe wasn't in his room, so William dropped his backpack off and set off down another hallway, partly wandering partly searching. He wasn't quite sure where to find Leila in the morning, but he figured he'd look.

As he passed the world language department, William spotted Cassie standing alone, typing away at her phone. She looked up, her eyes still drawn on heavily.

"Hey," William said, managing a smile.

"Hey, Will," she responded, directing her gaze downward again.

William figured it was better not to stick around. He walked down to the art room, entering his dim-lit, musty sanctuary. Mrs. Davis was slumped at her desk, stuck in her perpetual state of not giving a damn. William greeted her as warmly as he could.

"Morning, William," she responded, sitting up slowly. "How was your break?" She yawned.

"Not bad," he admitted. "You?"

"Eh," she said, not willing to reveal any more. "You need something?" Her eyes were tired and sagging, and William began to wonder if she got enough sleep.

"Um, I was just wondering if you'd seen Leila," he said, looking pointlessly around the room. He hadn't seen her since their adventure out of town that past Friday and curiosity was gnawing at his edges. Mrs. Davis told him she hadn't.

William waited around a minute after the bell rang, peeking his head out of the door to make sure the hallways were moderately clear before hurrying off to Mr. Monroe's room.

He ducked inside quickly, scurrying back to his seat before he was noticed more than he needed to be. Mr. Monroe had his back to the room, writing something up on the blackboard, the rest of the students in his class seemed to be milling about exchanging spring break stories. William clutched at the chain around his neck where a silver star of David hung, a treasure he had uncovered in his room the night he and his mom went back to synagogue.

"Hey, Will," Anthony said, taking the adjacent seat. He was adorned with one white ear bud, letting the other hang down lazily in front of him.

"Hey," William said, offering a smile. "How was break?" he asked out of habit.

"It was," Anthony responded, quickly running a pick through his hair. "Man, I was up 'til one working on that creative writing project." He laughed.

"Nice," William said, remembering the assignment that Mr. Monroe had given them earlier. He had entirely forgotten about it and had failed to realized that it had finally been assigned a due date, but a few chapters of his own work of fiction would probably suffice. "Yeah, I was getting pretty into mine," he admitted.

"I just can't do the whole writing thing," Anthony said over the sound of the late bell. This was hard for William to fathom.

"I like it," he said, honestly. "It's very…therapeutic."

Anthony shrugged. "Can I read yours?" he asked.

"Maybe later," William told him. *"When it's in print,"* he added to himself, smiling.

William found he was actually able to pay attention in class, given that his mind wasn't swarming with worry. He even raised his hand at one point when Mr. Monroe asked whether poetry was viewed as a form of art or just a means of complaining. William's response was long, fervent and heated.

Mr. Monroe ended class a few minutes later and called William, who was starting to pack his books away, up to his desk. The creative writing assignment had just been collected.

"I wanted to talk to you about your story," Mr. Monroe said, not to William's surprise. He motioned for William to pull up a chair.

"It's not really a serious thing," William lied. "Just, like, a spurt of creativity. I guess."

"I think you should keep working on it," Mr. Monroe stared down at him. "I think it's a project you should be willing to undertake. I've see a lot of potential in your writing even before this."

William sighed. "Honestly, the stuff I write for this class isn't supposed to be serious. I just do it for the grade. I even put *Fight Club* quotes in there," he admitted, embarrassed.

"Well if you aren't trying and it's still good, I have reason to believe you're a good writer," Mr. Monroe said with a laugh. "And yes, I've noticed the *Fight Club* quotes."

"I mean," William started, looking away. "It's just the beginning of the story; it doesn't really have anywhere to go. I don't have ideas. I don't think I have the time or mental stamina to write a book."

"So you think it could be a book?" Mr. Monroe asked excitedly.

"That's...no." William shook his head. "That's not what I meant." That was, in fact, exactly what William had meant.

"I think you can do it," Mr. Monroe said. "And I really want to see you succeed. I'll be willing to help you."

The bell rang, and William bit his lip, thinking hard.

"I..." he stopped. He couldn't abandon the story, no matter how little time he had to work on it. He couldn't say no, because Mr. Monroe believed in him, and he couldn't give up now, because he damn well wanted to write a book. "Would you help me edit?"

"Of course," his teacher told him, spinning around once in his chair. "Just bring me whatever else you've written and I'll look over it. This is yours, by the way," he said, handing William the chapters he had left over break. "I think you can do this, William." He propped his feet up on his desk.

William nodded. "Okay," he agreed. "Yeah, yeah. I think I probably could." He waited for Mr. Monroe to speak again, but he said nothing. "I, uh, have a few more parts I could bring you?" he continued hesitantly.

Mr. Monroe smiled. "Excellent," he said. "Do that. And stop calling them 'parts,' for Christ's sake. Chapters."

William nodded. "Chapters. Cool."

His teacher smiled in his quirky manner. "Don't let me down, kiddo."

"Don't count on it," William replied, but he smiled to show Mr. Monroe his dedication. He may not have believed in himself, but he had two very sensible people that did.

\* \* \*

William skimmed the rest of his day until fifth period, staring ever impatiently at the clock. The correlation, it seemed, between time and school was much lower than that of time and practically anything else. A fifty-five minute class seemed like a four hour lecture when you had no intention of remembering how to code a computer program. William had to remind himself every so often that minutes were precious and that he should not waste them. These reminders were half-assed efforts.

When he was finally released to the art room, William was welcomed by his favorite familiar scents and sounds. Soft grunge music floated from the radio that sat next to an idle Mrs. Davis, and the room was brightly lit and adorned with new Beatles posters. William slid into a seat at the back table, waiting for Leila, who was uncharacteristically late to arrive.

When she quietly shuffled in, it took William a moment to figure out what about her appearance had changed. Her hair was its signature fiery shade, and her face was bright but tired. She was dressed simply, as she often was, in a basic T-shirt.

A basic short-sleeved T-shirt.

It was seeing a person in bondage released from her chains; the ropes around her wrists untied. Though she huddled over, a little self-conscious, William couldn't help but smile.

The skin on her arms wasn't healed but it was beginning to, in that there were no new marks. There were faded pink and dull brown scars that seemed too many to count and the veins around her wrists were shallow and difficult to discern. Her skin wasn't pretty, but it was unbroken for what William knew was the first time in a long while.

"Hey," William said, as he pretended not to notice. Leila smiled over at him, unpacking a notebook and a few pencils.

"Afternoon," she replied, pleasantly. She knew that William had noticed and was not bothering to cover up her scars.

They didn't speak for a few minutes as they let Mrs. Davis ramble about putting the final touches on their abstract portraits, something that William had entirely forgotten about until now.

"You gotta really look inside you for this," Mrs. Davis was

saying, displaying more emotion in a few sentences than she had the entire year. "This isn't a painting of things you like or how people see you. It's the innermost part of your mind that you keep hidden. You're letting people see the stuff that's only viewable from the inside."

"She's getting real deep," William remarked in a hushed voice that only Leila could hear.

Leila smiled. "She's got a point though."

William shrugged and waited for Mrs. Davis to stop caring. He retrieved his portrait, almost complete but lacking closure. Racking his brain, he chomped on the end of a charcoal pencil for a way to finish. He looked over at Leila, who seemed to have suddenly thought up an enlightening idea and was passionately working away at something at the top corner of her canvas. When she finally picked her head up and looked back at William, she smiled.

"It's the dome," she said, pointing.

There it was, in all of its navy blue glory, formed at the top of Leila's painting from each end of the sky, towering protectively over Leila's pastel face. William couldn't suppress his smile.

"I told you I wasn't crazy," he said, gazing into Leila's intricate piece of art.

"I never thought you were," she admitted. "I just wanted to make sure that I wasn't."

William stared at her, at the honest words that were coming out of her mouth and the intelligent mind that had the sense to produce them. Her hands were Picasso and Monet and her mind was Thoreau, Vonnegut and Beethoven, and whoever else might be up there.

"I think I've decided that it doesn't hurt if it doesn't have to," she continued, no longer alluding to her brain. "And obviously, that starts with me."

William understood. "I like the short sleeves," he said, acknowledging her change. "It brings out your huge biceps."

"Shut up."

They smiled and worked in a peaceful silence. William finished his portrait with a figure in the sky sitting high up above William's head, past the clouds and the atmosphere in a blurred line that both existed and did not. He began to feel a new mass grow inside him, not weighing him down but instead giving him more person. He had helped someone find a reason to stop dragging a knife across her skin. He had cleared the smoke from her vision and she had showed him that she was grateful. And in turn, William felt something greater than satisfaction. William felt undeniable happiness.

# TWENTY-SEVEN

William was outside again for what would be the last time, at some hour that glanced between Friday night and Saturday morning. He had lost track of time sitting out on his back porch after his parents had gone to bed, scribbling thoughts in one of his old notebooks. The quiet ambiance of the night meant comfort, but he felt less at ease than normal. While he loved the nighttime, he was beginning to feel that it ought to be left alone.

William's green eyes strained through the fog and found his dome at the very tip of the sky. A crescent moon crossed his vision. He put his pen down, clutching at the Star of David around his neck, thinking of the repeat visit he and his mom had made to their synagogue earlier that night. Though, before the previous week, he hadn't been to his place of worship in at least seven years and he hardly had any idea what had been going on during the service, it all seemed familiar and welcoming, like the building and the congregation and the Torah itself had been patiently awaiting his return, whispering to him, "We're ready when you are." He felt a new belonging, the music still ringing in his ears.

He stepped off of the porch, wandering across the grass like a whisper. Subconsciously he was guided down the bike path toward his school, crossing over once stagnant creeks that now flowed musically without ceasing. Stepping off the path, William submerged himself in the profusion of trees, breathing in the scent of pine and rain. He walked to a sturdy looking oak and hauled himself up onto the lowest branch, climbing slowly, silently, as high as he could reach.

William perched on a sturdy limb, one hand wrapped around the tree's wide trunk to keep his balance. Gradually, he relaxed into a sitting position, carefully leaning back against the width of the tree until he could rest among the leaves. He shook slightly when he looked down, but kept one hand on a nearby branch for support. He closed his eyes and allowed his other senses to see for him.

William felt a pulse from deep within the tree, a heartbeat that started in the roots and spread all the way up to William's roost at the top. The almost unnoticeable, yet ever-present rhythm of the Earth was reaching for him, seeping into his hair and his skin and filling his ears with the steady cadence of nature. It was quiet and loud simultaneously. It was a heavenly peace and a stirring energy all at once. More than anything, it was comfort, like William was being cradled in the loving arms of his tree.

Reluctantly, William opened his eyes again and slowly began to climb back down, his feet lightly hitting the ground as he swung from the lowest branch. His skin tingled in the night air but an overwhelming tiredness began to nag at the back of his mind, telling him to go to bed, that he would need his energy. Rest seemed very appealing to him.

He began to make his way back home, pausing as he crossed a wooden bridge that passed over the singing creek. He leaned forward onto the railing, staring down at his darkened reflection. The water looked pure and clean, the air around him was soothing and cool. He felt very much at peace here, though torn by the idea of going back inside. He stayed for another moment, cherishing the fresh breeze and the sounds of living things around him.

William thought back to the frigid night that had led to a steel chain of moonlit walks and self doubt. He saw the drops of blood from his fist into the freshly-powdered snow, his shaking hands and the breath that froze before him. The feeling back then was desperation. The feeling now was more nostalgia than anything else.

A walk at midnight couldn't fix a broken mind; it could only organize some of the clutter. More often than not, the dark solitude of the sleeping streets did more harm than William intended; it left him alone with his thoughts, the ones that nipped at his brain and tugged on his heartstrings until he felt even worse than he had before. His mind was never clearer because he was alone, he was simply more aware. Aware of the good things with red hair and foster parents, and most prominently the bad things that took on all forms.

The midnight meanders were simply some old T-shirts that had shrunk in the dryer; William hadn't intended it, but he no longer fit into them, as he no longer fit inside his sleepy town. It was a soothing time and a peaceful setting but William didn't need the nighttime anymore.

There was a rustle in the leaves nearby and a wide-eyed fawn emerged, peering between the tree trunks with a fusion of caution and wonder. It gazed delicately at William, abandoning fear and instinct for simple curiosity. William stared back, both figures frozen in place by a silent understanding. Then, as silently and fluidly as it had approached, the fawn disappeared into the woods, and William was on his way again.

As he walked, he ran his fingers over the faded scars that embellished his knuckles, remembering clearly the feel of the frozen bark and the sore, stiff wind that had torn between his skin cells. It seemed a whole lifetime ago that William would have found it in him to punch a tree. The hostility of it frightened him even now and the lack of maturity he had felt at that moment was embarrassing to reminisce on, though it was an action not easily forgotten. Somehow, despite everything, it was not a regret.

William found himself in his backyard again, standing vulnerably in front of the tree that had suffered the consequences of his aggression.

"Sorry," he whispered, placing a hand on the coarse surface of the trunk out of sympathy. He felt the heartbeat once again and rested his head on the tree's thick skin.

William wondered what Leila was doing at that present

moment. She might have been drawing or listening to Bob Dylan or maybe reading a book. A week ago, she might have been dragging a knife across her wrist, silently watching a relentless stream of tears plummet from her cheeks. That no longer seemed likely. William felt it safe to assume that she was probably sleeping.

He felt a small pang of guilt all of a sudden, remembering what he had promised his mother on the way home from services that evening.

"So," she had asked him, flipping through a few quiet radio stations. "Can you promise me something?"

"Sure," William replied, curious.

"Can you promise me that you won't walk around at night anymore?" she asked, directing her full attention back on the road. "I'll help you find another coping mechanism, if that's what you need."

William was uneasy at first, contemplating the idea that his only means of escape would be taken from him. He agreed automatically, though his mind still dwelled on the thought.

"It's not like we live in a dangerous area," he had felt it necessary to add.

"Anywhere is a little dangerous at night," his mom said.

"Besides Canada," William interrupted.

His mother smiled. "Right. Besides Canada," she agreed. "But it's not just that. I'd just prefer it if you found a different way to deal with everything. You can stay inside and read or watch TV or do anything that clears your mind for a little while. Listen to music or play some stupid videogame if you have to," she told him. "Just stay inside at night. It can be lonely when you're out there on your own."

William had nodded in agreement.

*"This will be the last time,"* he decided presently, leaving his memory and standing back up, craning his neck to observe the stars.

He would miss the streetlamps that watched over him every night, shining through the fog and the rain and piercing through the darkness to guide him home. He would miss the sounds as well; cicadas humming gently beneath the rustle of leaves; undertones of the fluid motion of the creeks that flowed beneath him. The invigorating air that was only ever so refreshing at night.

He would particularly miss the comfort of the trees, the watchful guardians that saw all. He used to believe that they would never reveal their secrets; that insight into everything they observed, day and night, was unattainable. Leaning back against the trunk of his tree, however, William was beginning to realize the opposite. They would tell you their secrets if you promised to listen.

Reaching into one of his huge pockets, William pulled out his notebook again, clicking his pen twice before touching it to the paper. Fluidly, without the aid of any real thoughts, he wrote,

*"Your illness isn't you. Your family isn't you. Not even the rumors about you are really you. When you stand alone at night, entirely defenseless, and you see who you've been and who you are going to be, that's you all right. Your trials and defeats are woven together with your regrets and your dreams and your deepest fears. Your humility is thrown on top. Your beliefs are stitched in. That is who you are, and it is not a bad thing."*

*"Decent,"* William observed, silently crediting himself. He had gone so long believing he was talentless; everyone he knew had *something* going for them, whether it be a specific academic interest or musical talent. While he was an able athlete, William didn't expect to play soccer in college, certainly not at a division one school. He was a good student, but no valedictorian. He had never considered writing to be the thing that set him apart.

But a writer, he had begun to realize, had no less talent than a biochemist. What William lacked in aptitude for math or science, he made up for otherwise.

*"How good would it look on a college application if I wrote a book?"* he thought, suddenly. The thought did not take much stimulation to grow, and soon William, who had never expected his story of Ross and Edwin to amount to anything, was quickly submerged in ideas and prospects. Mr. Monroe believed he could write it, Leila believed he could finish it. William just needed to believe he could pursue it.

*"Well, shit,"* he thought. *"I'm going to write a book."*

At that moment, William discovered what some might call purpose, and he liked it. He knew it wouldn't be an easy task, figuring it very likely that no real success would come from a teenager's attempt to write a novel. Nevertheless, he had finally stopped spinning around every bearing and was finally facing the right direction.

The path in front of him was difficult to discern, overgrown with bushes and thorns, barely even noticeable with the exception of a few footsteps that proved to lead the way. That night, William had stepped onto this path, unable to see where it ended but knowing he wanted to walk along it. At the edges were all of the things that moved him: tall trees to listen when he was troubled, streetlamps to pierce the darkness that might hinder him. A kind friend with red hair to walk with him when he felt alone.

That seemed enough motivation in itself.

William walked back to the spot on his porch where he first began to find himself a week ago. He looked to the sky the same way he had before and he felt the same feelings, saw the same graceful arc of the atmosphere above him.

"Thank you," William whispered again. He turned back to his house and walked inside, casting one last glance at the midnight sky before quietly shutting the door behind him.

**LODESTONE
BOOKS**

Lodestone Books is a new imprint, which offers a broad
spectrum of subjects in YA/NA literature. Compelling reading,
the Teen/Young/New Adult reader is sure to find something
edgy, enticing and innovative. From dystopian societies, through
a whole range of fantasy, horror, science fiction and paranormal
fiction, all the way to the other end of the sphere, historical
drama, steam-punk adventure, and everything in between.
You'll find stories of crime, coming of age and contemporary
romance. Whatever your preference you will discover it here.